MW00719235

Travelers' Tales

Travelers' Tales

Michael Newton

2010
Galde Press
Lakeville, Minnesota, U.S.A.

Travelers' Tales
© Copyright 2003 by Michael Duff Newton
All rights reserved.
Printed in the United States of America
No part of this book may be used or
reproduced in any manner whatsoever
without written permission from the pub-
lishers except in the case of brief
quotations embodied in critical articles
and reviews.

Second Edition
Third Printing, 2010

Cover photograph by Rick Sammon

Library of Congress Cataloging-in-Publication Data

Newton, Michael, 1931-
  Travelers' tales / Michael Newton.— 1st ed.
    p. cm.
  ISBN 1-931942-02-1
  1. Self-actualization (Psychology)—Fiction. 2. Psychological
fiction, American. I. Title.
  PS3614.E76T73 2003
  813'.6—dc21

                                        2003002540

Galde Press
PO Box 460
Lakeville, Minnesota 55044–0460

Dedication

To Peggy, Kathryn and Norah,
my wife, daughter and sister,
the three most important
women in my life, who have had
to endure my stories over so
many years.

Table of Contents

Preface

With the exception of my science fiction story about future space travelers called "Finite," all the tales set in overseas locations within this collection are based to a greater or lesser extent upon truth. Still, they too must be classified as fiction.

Elements of the plot in the first story, "The Porcelain Dragons," came from my father's experiences as a U.S. vice-consul in Kobe, Japan, during the early 1920s. The other seven stories entail physical and emotional challenges to the human spirit in settings where I have had some degree of personal involvement in my travels around the world.

The Porcelain Dragons

TICKETS, SIR!" The Japanese train conductor said, as he braced himself against an arm rest for balance and extended his hand toward John Bowmont.

Staring moodily out the window, the distinguished looking American seemed not to hear. Bowmont's wife Martha fished out two stubs from her coat and the official moved away.

"Aren't these accommodations luxurious, dear?" she sighed happily, reclining against her chair of soft fabric in the pressurized coach. Martha reached over and squeezed her husband's fingers.

"Yes, yes…" he mumbled in acknowledgement, his expression solemn, still detached in thought. Bowmont's light gabardine suit was already rumpled as he shifted his long, bony body around to a new position. The old leg injury was bothering him again.

The sleek Tokaido Express accelerated noiselessly on the three-hundred mile race to Osaka where they would transfer to Kobe. As the landscape outside rapidly blurred, Bowmont saw only his reflection mirrored within the cold, stainless steel bordered window. Under a shock of straight white hair, a thin, anguished face glared back, ghost-like, mocking him. Bowmont had not been well for a long time. Quite a grotesque alteration, he mused, from that bright-eyed, eager young diplomat who stepped off the steamship *President Adams* in Yokohama. It was

1

the summer of 1919 at the entrance to a strange, mysterious land. He had been gone for forty years and now, at last, he was back.

Bowmont glanced again at his wife. Martha was a large, imposing woman of Scandinavian ancestry, her appearance incongruous with the Japanese passengers sitting near them. Self-assured, kind, but very shrewd he thought without rancor. Martha looked up from her book. "Try taking a nap, John," she turned and smiled gently at him. "I'll keep an eye on things." She always does, thankfully, he reminded himself.

Bowmont had met his wife in Minneapolis a year after his leg was crippled by a collapsing wall while engaging in the rescue operations during Japan's great earthquake of 1923. The injury forced his retirement as a vice-consul from the American Foreign Service. Martha was the child of a wealthy industrialist. Although devoted to Bowmont, her perspective about life was quite different from his own. He attributed this partly to an excess of family money.

After their marriage, Bowmont had accepted an offer from his new father-in-law to manage a department in one of his machinery plants. Bowmont wasn't particularly suited for the job, but he stuck it out. Practical, and endowed with her father's head for business, Martha was a great asset, counterbalancing his own romantic soul. Despite their minor rivalries, he grew to depend upon her in the dreary years of corporate life which followed, and the bond between them grew strong.

The trip to Japan was initially Martha's idea. She had never been to the Far East and wanted to go with him. At first Bowmont had resisted her prodding, afraid of breaking the seal containing his precious memories of those five golden years of his life—unlocking them to her and the impurities of a newer age. His wife finally said, rather bluntly, that he should return to recapture the one bright spot in his life while there was still time. Deep inside, Bowmont was motivated by a desire for Martha to see him in control in an environment unfamilir to her. Eventually, he agreed to come.

Now, he was convinced it was all a mistake. Flying into the suffocating crush of Tokyo's megalopolis, Bowmont's sensibilities were overwhelmed. Staring blankly out the railway car window, he cringed in his seat at the picture of Tokyo's giant elevated highways, solid blocks of concrete high-rise and cantilevered girders supporting every conceivable shape of advertising. The capital was a jungle of clubs, junk stands and crowded humanity held in the grip of total commercialism. This wasn't his Japan. When Bowmont could take no more he cancelled the balance of their hotel reservation and left Tokyo for what he hoped would be the recovery of better memories associated with his former diplomatic post at Kobe.

The train rocketed on. "How much longer to Kobe?" Martha asked the conductor who was making his rounds down the aisle.

"Two more hours to Osaka. Another half-hour to Kobe," the conductor answered over his shoulder.

Bowmont's mind returned to the train. "God, it used to take all night!"

"And you expected they'd still be using rickshaws in the streets," Martha laughed. "Cheer up John, you'll soon be around your old haunts in Kobe."

"I'm almost afraid to see Kobe again," Bowmont sighed, squirming in his seat.

Martha glanced at his face and it saddened her to see his apprehension, even resistance. She said, "Well, naturally things are a bit different, dear. Probably far more civilized since the end of the war and our occupation, if you ask me."

"Of course you approve of this frenzied emulation of American society?" Bowmont muttered dismissively.

"Japan seems very industrious and booming," she replied evenly. "After all, our country is a model for any nation...democratic, educated, clean..."

"And sterile—as far as the Orient is concerned," he rasped angrily. Bowmont felt a knot in the pit of his stomach. "Sure, that's the idea, I guess, white-wash everyone over in our image. Take away their history, culture, language..."

Martha did not want to provoke him further. She took up her book again while Bowmont slumped against the window, mesmerized by the train's vibration and the mournful plunking of Samisen music piped in over their heads.

Bowmont's thoughts returned to his last days in Japan at the end of August, 1923. He was in Yokohama at the evening wedding of his close friend Hugh Magnum. The event was vivid in Bowmont's mind, even today, because it climaxed his early life. The following morning his age of innocence was over with the ground coming apart under him, the terror of falling buildings, the screams of his friends, of the pain and death from one of the most devastating earthquakes of the century.

He wrenched his mind away from the horrors of the quake, back to the blissful wedding reception, his own toast to the bride and Magnum's special gift to his new wife. Suddenly, Bowmont's body shook with laughter.

"What's so funny, dear." Martha's hand was on his sleeve.

"Oh, I was just thinking of my friend, Hugh Magnum."

Martha was glad to see her husband out of his doldrums.

"You've mentioned him before—about being together a lot?"

"Yes, we were," he said. Then Bowmont began to talk, the words pouring out. "Magnum was a medical doctor for our American colony in Kobe. He was considered an eccentric, but his perception of Japanese philosophy was uncanny. The man was a scholar of sorts with Asian art, collecting antiques in his spare time—particularly Japanese Imari porcelain."

"Chinaware, you mean?"

"Yes, but not the cluttered, thick stuff we saw on Tokyo's main streets. You can buy that trash anywhere. Magnum had made a study of the factory locations producing the finest Imari china in early Japan, under the patronage of feudal lords. You see, before 1853 only the Dutch were allowed to trade in Japanese ceramics, through the single port of Nagasaki. The foreign demand was high, since the the glaze and painting process used by those artisans was a closely guarded secret."

"I see," she said, waiting, not comprehending where all this was going.

"To get away from the city, I often accompanied Magnum on his weekend excursions," Bowmont continued, warming to his subject. "One day we chanced to stop at an isolated village where there was a shop. The owner, an old man called Shigeru, was aloof and distrusted foreigners because he dealt with so few of us. On a shelf, collecting dust, Magnum spied a large platter of Imari china. Taking it down carefully, he explained it was a valuable relic of late-eighteenth century porcelain. It was beautiful, Martha. In the center of the platter was a powerful design…an iron-red dragon, with a simple foliated border of the same color surrounding the plate, delicately traced under a cream-white paste."

"Mmm...sounds very nice, John," she said patiently. Martha labeled the page she was reading and closed her book. She had little conception of what he was talking about. Bowmont was oblivious to this, while he surged on, the words tumbling out.

"Anyway, when Magnum finished his investigation of the markings, I became as excited as he was over our find. But instead of discussing the china, Magnum proceeded to compliment Shigeru on living in such a picturesque area of Japan. They talked about the climate, the Emperor, America—until I was ready to burst from anticipation."

"Then, at last, Magnum gingerly asked if there might be any more pieces to the set. 'It is possible,' Shigeru said. We both realized there was more. Magnum's demeanor was relaxed, but I was still inexperienced in Japanese customs. 'We want to buy whatever you have,' I blurted out rashly."

"The old-fashioned shopkeeper froze and Magnum shuddered at my temerity. Shigeru was so offended a foreigner would brazenly try to rush him into a transaction of Imari ware he wanted nothing more to do with either of us. Going home, Magnum was very upset with me. He said it would probably take him a year to cultivate the venerable store owner to a point where he might be willing to sell the set of Imari china. We made a bet."

"What kind of bet?" Martha inquired.

"I wagered Magnum a case of Scotch whisky he was wrong and that Shigeru would sell all the Imari ware at once, if the price was right. I didn't tell Magnum but I decided to go back to the shop by myself."

"And what happened?"

"For months I tried off and on but I got nowhere with old Shigeru, although I learned a great deal about Japanese customs. Eventually, I gave up my quest.

"Did your friend ever get the china?"

"Over a year later our group at the consulate left Kobe for Yokohama to attend Magnum's wedding. The couple was sailing home to the States on their honeymoon. At the reception that night Magnum had the hotel staff bring in a number of large boxes as a present for his bride. With elaborate fanfare, he motioned me to come over and stand next to her while she unwrapped the first box. The boxes contained around eighty pieces of the dragon set. I was dumfounded. As the story circulated around the dining room, there was much joking at my expense."

"His income was, no doubt, higher than yours," Martha observed dryly.

"No, no, you don't understand, Martha. As I remember, the price was ridiculously low, even for those days. But Magnum had painstakingly collected the set in his own way from Shigeru a few pieces at a time."

"It sounds rather tedious, John," she smiled indulgently, "I mean…"

"Oh, it doesn't matter," Bowmont cut in, disgusted with her. "Early the next morning the Grand Hotel was ripped apart by the quake. The fire destroyed everything, including Magnum and his wife. I was out of the building taking a walk."

"How tragic!" Martha exclaimed. Her body shivered. "You've never told me this before. What a blessing you weren't there."

"Maybe," he said quietly.

Along the aisles of the train, a kimono-clad siren, eye folds widened by plastic surgery, passed out refreshments. Martha signaled the hostess and, with a flurry of swaying hips, the girl delivered two watered-down drinks, collecting a large tab.

Later, as they drew into Kobe, an inner excitement swelled up inside Bowmont. Recollections of consulate parties, mountain hikes to the bubbling hot springs of Mount Rokho, sailing under a pale moon across the Inland Sea to Kobe's off-shore islands topped with pines, flowed through his mind.

However, Bowmont's first view of the raw, explosive energy generated by the modern port city of Kobe numbed him. Nothing is the same, he thought hopelessly.

They left the train and caught a cab to the Oriental Hotel. Bowmont asked to be driven by his former consulate. It was gone, replaced by a new building.

"We stop?" The driver asked.

"No, dammit—just go on to the hotel," Bowmont cried. "I suppose it's brand new as well."

"Yes! Sixty percent of city destroyed by Allied bombs," the driver spieled off. "We rebuild, better than before. Million people live here now. Like Tokyo, very nice—no?"

The cab squealed to a halt. "Twenty dollar," the driver commanded. Jumping out of the car, he hurriedly dropped their bags on the curb.

"How much?" Bowmont grumbled. They had only gone a short distance from the train station.

Martha paid him and the car careened off down the street narrowly missing a motorcycle rider.

Bowmont heard purposeful riveting, and looking around, he saw relentless bulldozers stripping the city of its remaining past, burying it under masses of dirt. After they checked into the hotel,

Martha decided to rest while Bowmont spent a few hours searching the streets for something recognizable. There were shiny new department stores, industrial plants, hotels and more hotels. He asked local residents about people he had known with no success. He decided they were all gone or dead. It's hard to give up, he thought, so many miles to get here—a wasted lifetime behind.

Walking slowly and leaning heavily on his cane, Bowmont returned to the hotel lobby. "Can I rent a car for a side trip tomorrow?" he inquired at the desk.

"Yes," the clerk answered, "but I do not recommend it."

"Why not?"

"The roads away from the cities can be difficult for tourists alone. English is only occasionally spoken in some rural areas. If you are not acquainted with this region…"

"I know the area," Bowmont replied curtly in Japanese. "I want you to arrange for a car tomorrow morning."

"Yes sir," the astonished clerk acknowledged.

The next morning a light rain was falling as Bowmont and his wife got into their car. Martha's naturally curly, short hair glistened with the dampness.

"John, it's not a particularly good day. Where are we going?"

Bowmont looked at his wife with a kind of desperation. "I'm not sure, really. Towards Nara maybe. It's a scenic drive…" Abruptly, he clasped her arms, placing his lips on her cheek, then he looked into her eyes.

"Martha, its important to me that you see something of the beauty and elegance of what I remember. I've got to get away from the cities. There has to be something left for me—something I can recapture…"

The road to Nara, capitol of Japan in the eighth century, was humid but breathtaking with the bloom of late spring. There was an intermittent sun behind a cloudy sky. Kobe and Osaka were well behind them when the fields of rice paddies and closely-tilled farms gave way to gently rolling slopes. The car climbed past a land of yellow mustard and sprouting barley, and soon there was a carpet of green which lay over terraced hills, patched by primeval forests of gnarled pine and black cedar. Occasionally, they saw small dwellings with thatched roofs and he began to feel a little better. His faith in the adopted country of his early manhood was being reborn again by its soil.

At noon, the couple entered legendary Nara under majestically timbered gates. They chose to have lunch on a bench next to the polished arches of the sacred Todaiji Temple.

"Ladies and gentleman," the sonorous voice of a tour leader holding a megaphone announced, "here is the hall of the Great Buddha, over a thousand years old, housing the largest bronze statue in the world."

Bowmont stared up again at the perpetual, enigmatic smile of the five-hundred ton figure he had so often regarded in the relative quietude of this garden park long ago.

Now the walkways were packed with tourists. Babies wailed in their carriages, lovers sprawled on the lawn, and venders blatantly peddled a variety of junk curios, fast food and soft drinks. Bowmont was not mindful of the crowd's enjoyment. He saw only a tawdry tourist attraction. The tranquilizing enlightenment of Nara's benevolent Buddha was wasted on these people, he thought. He felt the sense of loss gnawing away at him once more.

After they finished their sandwiches brought from the hotel, Bowmont hurried his wife away from the crowded park. An idea, slowly growing inside him for many hours, had crystallized, coming to the surface of his conscious mind as if by sudden impulse.

"Martha, I'm going to find that village!"

"What village?"

"Where Shigeru's shop was located. I remember that it's in a valley not far from here, to the north on the Kyoto road. I'd like to…look for it."

There was a rumbling in the sky. Martha was edgy and her temper flared. "John, I don't think it is possible for you to be content here with anything. Do you expect to discover a slumbering Brigadoon waiting for you after all these years? I'm concerned about the weather; it's turning nasty."

"Come on," he said decisively, "it won't take long." Bowmont started the car with a flash of self-pride, seeing Martha uncharacteristically ruffled, not realizing her concern was largely for him.

Within the next half hour the thunder was replaced by a steady drizzle. The narrow roadway through the hills grew slippery and Martha became more apprehensive. "John, is it so important that you locate this store? I mean, the place was probably torn down ages ago."

"I'll find it. I'm sure things haven't changed that much out here in the countryside," he answered, driving as if possessed.

Bowmont's pulse quickened with an insatiable desire to find Shigeru's store. He knew Shigeru was long dead and that the store had taken on an unnatural significance for him, yet he couldn't help himself. Bowmont felt this pilgrimage to rural Japan was his last chance for a tangible link to the past.

Soon a small settlement came into view. They crossed a vermillion-colored bridge spanning a meandering stream and were carried into a lush, peaceful valley.

"There it is! Over there. Look, Martha—do you see it?" Bowmont cried, pointing at the hazy outline of a square structure silhouetted through the veil of rain. "Still here, after all this time. I knew it! Now, Martha, you'll see something of the old, unspoiled Japan," he cried excitedly, turning the car into a graveled driveway.

However, the store was not the same. Bowmont noticed the miniature Zen shrine was still nestled in a clump of bamboo, adjacent to the walkway. But the store itself had been remodeled with a shoji screen front, sliding panels and a wide, freshly lacquered porch flanked by paper lanterns. There was also a house in back.

"Is this what we came to see?" Martha looked closely at her husband.

"Yes…" Bowmont said, disconcerted for a moment. He got out slowly, his bad leg stiff from the drive. Taking his wife's arm, he limped alongside her to the steps.

Then, Bowmont underwent a transformation. The years rolled away and it was not his wife, but Magnum climbing beside him up the stone steps of the old building. They were in high spirits, flushed by the adventure of another day's exploration. As the screen door was pushed open, Shigeru filled Bowmont's mind; the half-bent shuffle, his weathered face, etched by deep lines and coal-black eyes keenly appraising the two young Americans.

"Hi folks!" A sing-song falsetto greeting evaporated Bowmont's mood of reverie. "Looking for a nice souvenir? I help you pick out something—okay?"

Bowmont shook himself. It was not Shigeru, but a skinny, thoroughly westernized Japanese boy who stood before them. There was a cocky smugness about the youth that his superficial smile did not conceal. Raucous streams of rock and roll emitted from a transistor radio at his belt.

Martha and her husband saw the store's inventory was a hodgepodge of ordinary jewelry, silk shirts, inferior wood carvings, parasols, inexpensive pottery and stacks of modern Japanese prints. "Is this the store of Shigeru?" Bowmont inquired gravely, the enchantment broken.

For a moment the condescending smile left the youth. "Yes, he was my grandfather," he replied with surprise, turning off the radio.

"I...knew him," Bowmont declared.

The boy recovered his wits. "Yep, he has long ago joined his worthy ancestors. But don't worry, I take good care of you. Since the war, my father's health very bad. I mostly run shop now," he stated blithely.

The youth measured the Bowmonts with a practiced eye. Who are these fogies, he pondered. The man is not the usual article. Someday I'll get out of this hut and have my own store in Osaka with a real tourist trade.

Bowmont took in a deep breath. "A long time ago your grandfather sold a number of Imari tableware pieces to a friend of mine—in fact I used to come here myself. Red and white it was. I...I wanted to see the store again...," he broke off lamely.

The young man nonchalantly leaned back against the counter. His expression did not change, making it harder on Bowmont. What kind of pigeon is this, the boy wondered.

Martha sensed her husband's disorientation. He's perplexed and doesn't know how to proceed, she thought with compassion. She'd cut this upstart down to size in short order. "Do you have any early Japanese china left in this place?" she demanded loudly.

"Imari ware?" the young man rubbed his chin. "Is that what you want?"

"Yes," she said impatiently, "Is there any in the store?"

Speechless, Bowmont stared at his wife. How artless of her. Of course there was no Imari ware lying around. It was rare forty years ago. Lord, did she think she could just walk in and...

"Wait a minute!" the boy said, frowning. Hastily, he retreated to a storage area adjacent to the back room. The Bowmonts could hear a frantic rustling of paper and the creaking of disturbed wooden crates. The boy returned with a battered tea box in his arms, strips of yellowed paper hung out of the cracked sides.

"I was cleaning out stock a few weeks ago and found this," the boy puffed, setting the box on the counter. "Let's take a peek," he said, tossing bits of straw and paper on the floor. And there, in front of the ex-consul, a vision locked in a former reality suddenly came to life in the deft hands of this callous youth.

"My God—Martha," Bowmont gasped, "it isn't all gone!"

Tears squeezed out his eyes as he helped the boy lift out a teapot, cups, saucers, one bowl and a platter until there were eleven pieces. Coiled eternally across each one, scaled and prickled like a crocodile, the three-clawed red dragons glowered up at Bowmont from their monstrous heads once again. He felt the presence of Magnum standing beside him.

Nostalgically turning over the china, Bowmont's hands quivered. "Do you see, Martha," he said eagerly, "the same roughened kiln marks on each piece. It's caused by clay spurs upon which the porcelain rested during firing."

One look at her husband fondling the china was enough for Martha. Up to now she had been unable to reach his troubled mind. Here was a tangible thing to make him happy. She would make his trip worthwhile. They could never use these odd pieces from an old dish set, but it mattered to John and she was going to have it for him.

"Is this all you have?" Martha queried the Japanese boy disparagingly.

"That's the lot." The boy sized up his adversary, while Martha measured him. There was an immediate business rapport between them.

"This china is small, incomplete—unusable actually, you realize that," she said in an off-handed tone.

"Lady, you and I both know these goods don't grow on trees," the boy shot back.

The rain increased, beating heavily on the corrugated tin roof. Bowmont awoke from his trance and became aware of the bargaining.

"All right," Martha's voice was brittle, "name your price." She unlatched her purse. "How much for the lot?"

"Four hundred dollars," the boy pronounced extending his arm, palm open.

Bowmont was horrified. What were they doing? Such an insult to the memory of Shigeru. We have descended to the lowest point on this trip, he thought. He was witnessing a final act of contempt by Japan's inheritors. His mouth opened in protest.

"Robbery, and you know it!" Martha retorted, leaning towards the boy, her lips firmly compressed. "I'll give you exactly two hundred cash—not a penny more." She peeled off two bills, estimating the boy would probably pocket at least one for himself.

The boy hesitated for an instant, calculating. "For three even we got a deal," he negotiated dryly.

Bowmont's shoulders sagged, he felt helpless.

The store was invaded by the sound of splashing water as a back door swung wide and slammed shut. A Japanese man, prematurely old, approached the counter slowly. One side of his face was badly scarred by shell fragments from the war.

"Everything all right?" he sternly inquired of the boy.

"Yes, esteemed father," the boy's manner abruptly became defensive.

The man angrily surveyed the china strewn around his counter and addressed the Bowmonts. "I sincerely hope my son has told you these articles are not for sale."

"Of course," Bowmont exclaimed in triumph. "It was evident to me these few pieces come from a priceless family heirloom. It's a privilege just to look at them."

Martha remained silent, scowling fiercely at the boy who gulped in frustration. "This gentleman knew grandfather," he said at last, shrinking back to one end of the counter.

"Oh so?" The Japanese man said, his countenance inscrutable.

"That's true," Bowmont said easily. "Years ago I came to your store. This porcelain was fired at the Arita kilns in Hizen province, wasn't it?"

"Yes, they were,'" the man acknowledged, regarding Bowmont intently.

Bowmont carefully picked up a bowl and held it up high.

"One has only to observe the translucent enamel surface glaze to know the quality," he continued.

The Japanese man brightened a little. "My name is Okano. I can see you are a connoisseur of fine china, sir."

"Well, to tell the truth I was educated by a mutual friend of your father and I have seen this particular set before. Your son has just materialized a part of my life I thought was extinct."

Bowmont introduced himself and his wife and briefly related the facts of Magnum's visits and his Imari purchases from Shigeru.

"Then we are doubly honored by your return visit to our humble shop after so long an absence," Okano said cordially. Decisively, he motioned his son away from the counter and said, "Mrs. Bowmont, I hope you and your husband will honor us by staying awhile and allowing us to serve hot tea and rice cakes on this damp afternoon?"

During the next hour, in a private alcove, Martha and the boy spoke little while the two men conversed, often in Japanese. At last Okano and Bowmont rose from the floor cushions and bowed low to each other.

"There isn't much left of the old things we knew, is there?" Bowmont remarked wistfully.

"My friend, it is easy to become disillusioned," Okano answered, his round, myopic features thoughtful. "But our island heritage has survived much in its long history. It will not die. As a man who knew what was here before, you can see we may have lost some identity with our past. There is a spiritual void that easy living does not accommodate. I believe I know how you feel, Mr. Bowmont. I also have had to come to terms with my nation's compulsion for mass production of bright gadgets. We can not return to the past, and there is much that is good today. We are no longer a militaristic nation. Our people are prosperous with new ideas and they have more personal freedom than we did. In time, when our young realize their world of material values does not give them fulfillment, perhaps some of the old ways that were honorable will be accepted again and give them strength of character. It is the task—no, the duty—of our generation to guide them."

Bowmont and his Japanese host ceremoniously prepared to take leave of each other. Martha saw the glow in her husband's esthetic face and she was gratified.

"How many pieces of the dragon set do we have left?" Okano asked his son casually.

"Just what is here father," the boy said, startled.

Martha stopped at the counter and unstrapped her purse again. She registered a faint, knowing smile of satisfaction.

"Fine," Okano said, "please wrap all the pieces up carefully for the Bowmonts' long journey home."

The boy paused by the cash register, still confused, waiting.

His father spoke with serene patience.

"As a gift to our guests, my son."

Beldame of Bruges

I T WAS BITTERLY COLD when the young American turned down the last narrow cobblestone street leading to the chapel. Under a darkening sky, the wind-driven misty rain whipped the loose slacks about his long, thin legs. He stepped forward with uncertainty. It was slippery along the antique, roughly cut walkway and he needed to take care. As a student of history, the American was visiting Europe and the places he had read about for the first time. Only a few weeks from home, he had arrived just that morning at the medieval city of Bruges.

The city fascinated him almost to the point of awe. He thought of himself as a time traveler from the future while threading his way past the small, quaint shops and winding canals of this preserved city. World War II had not been over for long and many of Europe's cities were still in ruins, yet this vestige of the Middle Ages in Belgium had been spared.

The young man was still unaccustomed to being called a foreigner. The realization of this had been evident a short while ago when he asked directions to this particular church from a wrinkled, badly-stooped old woman dressed all in black. With a leering, grotesque half-smile, she had cocked her head at him and rasped, "You foreigners always have trouble finding your way round our quiet town." She seemed hostile, and perhaps her

19

attitude that he was an intruder stemmed from living through the painful years of a devastating war. He didn't know.

His step quickened as he came at last to the entrance of the chapel he was seeking, known for five centuries as Our Lady's Church. The American pushed open the heavy oak doors and stepped into an age of chivalry. Below the ceiling hung a musty array of vivid battle flags, trophies of untold clashes of armor and men. He examined the rich silk patterns of red and black lions emblazoned on some of the banners. He knew these to be the armorial bearings of the Counts of Flanders and the great Dukes of Burgundy. Across the walls under the flags, still in glorious color, stood the heraldic shields of thirty knights of the Order of the Golden Fleece. The young man remembered from his classes that the original knights of this illustrious group were only a generation old when Charles the Bold ascended to the Duchy of Burgundy in the the fifteenth century at the zenith of its power.

After gazing for some time at these relics of medieval splendor, the young man passed into a bare, low-vaulted antechamber. In the center of this room he looked closely at two heavy stone coffins, side by side, one large and other quite small. These contained the remains of Duke Charles and his young daughter, Mary, the last members of their Burgundian line.

Over the coffins, two marble lids were beautifully carved with the effigies of father and daughter as they had looked in life. The young man paused over the figure of Mary. Gently, he traced his fingers over the girl's exquisite features forever etched in pale marble. She had died in the spring of her youth, close to his own age. While he touched her face, Mary came alive for the American, beckoning him in the silence to be with her in her own century.

There was the mournful sound of a bell in the distance and the spell was broken. The young man became aware of a frigid atmosphere in the chapel and realized it was growing late. He walked slowly out a side door into an adjoining graveyard. The twilight held the young man in a pall of gloom. Hands shivering, he wrapped a wool scarf more tightly around his neck as the dampness penetrated into his lean body. A cold wind whistled between the irregular headstones scattered in the graveyard everywhere about him, and they too served as monuments of the past. Across a willow-covered canal bridge, the sad tolling of the old belfry tower added to the American's reverie of a bygone age.

Suddenly, down the darkened path behind him, a shadow swept past, stopped and twisted around. The young man was startled, his senses only half in the present. He slowed his pace. With his tear-laden eyes still blurred from the communion with Mary, he perceived a chalk-white face, shrouded in black lace, glaring back at him.

"So! This is how you treat a friend?" screeched the apparition.

Dazed, the young man did not comprehend. He looked dumbly at the crone's disheveled gray hair and her prominent chin jutting aggressively out at him, but his mind was still not fully back in his own time. A sense of dread crept over him and he was unable to speak.

"Fie on you! Haughty boy—bad boy!" she hissed vehemently, shaking a bony finger at him and moving closer.

The young man stared in horror at the witch in front of him in this ominous setting. All his constrained nervous emotion exploded at once. With the uncontrolled fleetness of a deer, he raced to the low stone wall bordering the church yard, hurled himself over and ran wildly into the street. Gasping, his head finally cleared and only then did he recognize the witch as the old woman who had given him directions earlier in town. He recoiled at his foolishness.

Pathways and Poppies

E VERYTHING WAS EMERALD GREEN. The steamy brilliance of the humid jungle was alive with a perpetual, high-pitched buzzing from flying clouds of flies and mosquitoes. A thick, sweetly-scented landscape formed an envelope around the party of ten people hiking in single file along a broken trail in Northwest Thailand. Eight of the ten were Western tourists, who looked awkward and out of place as they hacked their way through the lush foliage with machetes. The rutted path, often indistinct, led the party in the direction of the Burmese border.

They were now some fifty miles west of the Thai town of Chiang Mai, having been trucked in to a starting point about ten miles back. It was only the afternoon of the first day and already Ellen felt sorry she had allowed herself to be talked into this excursion by a well-meaning friend. She had been reluctant to come. "You can't say you've really seen Thailand without doing a tribal trek to visit the hill people," her friend had admonished. The experience was already proving to be a hot, dirty and even humiliating exercise for her. She watched the others in front hacking away at the undergrowth blocking the trail and had the impression they actually relished the sweaty effort required of them.

As the party pushed their way along the trail in back of Min, leader of the trek, Ellen thought she was simply not so adventurous

as the rest. She also considered that a vacation to this part of the
world was probably a mistake. As the day wore on, sweat ran
down her forehead in one continuous stream. She wiped the moisture away with the back of her hand for the hundredth time and
wondered why she hadn't the sense to bring a bandanna. Ellen
found that although her thick hair was cut short, it was sticky
and hopelessly tangled around pieces of brush. And this is supposed to be fun, she thought to herself.

The party began moving through a dense wedge of sharp bamboo stalks near a canal filled with reeds and muddy water. The
bamboo relentlessly whipped at her body while Ellen struggled
up an incline. She had stumbled a few times in the bamboo forest and realized that her new blouse was stained. The designer
jeans she wore were filthy from red clay mixed with the rain water
that had intermittently lashed down upon the trekkers all day.
The group came to a gap in the forest where the going was easier, and Ellen's thoughts drifted away from the trail.

Within her own element, Ellen pictured herself as a confident
business woman who was a driver rather than a spectator. In her
late twenties, with one broken engagement and disillusionment
in her personal life, she was finally gaining respect professional-
ly as an architect. It gave her some satisfaction to know she was
dependent upon no one for either economic or emotional support.
The fighting for recognition in a competitive field had honed her
personality into one of toughness and resilience, although she was
not particularly happy. Ellen stumped along the trail reflecting
upon the obstacles she had overcome in the past by stubbornly
covering up her deeper feelings. Because she never wanted to
miplace her loyalties again, she did not trust herself anymore with
men who attempted to get close.

As the gap in the bamboo forest ended, her mind returned to the task at hand. Min now shifted the positions of various members of the party and Ellen found herself placed near the head of the line where the work was harder.

"Careful now!" the man in front of her shouted back, "this next grove of bamboo is going to be tough to get through."

Ellen didn't respond. His name was Brian something or other, she thought. The reason she knew this was because he was the only other American on the trek. She supposed he was trying to be helpful and yet his obvious pleasure at all the hard labor only annoyed her further.

Brian's shirt was tied around his waist, and Ellen saw the cords of his hard back muscles shift up and down while he swung the machete blade as if it were a sword. She noticed his body coordination during the blade swings. Brian's rhythm was almost casual in the natural way he utilized energy. In the last few hours he had become quite proficient with the unfamiliar machete. The fool was actually enjoying himself, Ellen mused, knowing she was working much too hard for the results she was getting in return. She badly wanted to stop for a drink and some rest, but that would slow up everyone else. Min set the pace and the rest breaks. He had told the group after lunch they were behind schedule in reaching the first village.

Suddenly, there was an abrupt drop in the trail and she fell to her knees. Hearing her swear, Brian stopped and turned around. He took Ellen's arm and carefully helped her up.

"You okay?" His voice was level and, she imagined, a shade critical.

"Are you getting tired?" he said casually.

Ellen's stomach knotted in anger. "No, dammit!" she snapped at him defensively, blood rushing to her face. "Just go on."

She saw the man was taken aback. He was lightly bearded, and the reddish hairs, closely trimmed on his square, uncomplicated face glistened with sweat. She felt heavy beads of moisture dropping off his face on her while he still firmly held her arm.

"You sure?" the man asked again, smiling. His easy familiarity toward her difficulties only grated on her more.

"Yes, I said so, didn't I!" Ellen's tone sounded shrill even to herself as she pulled her arm away from his grasp.

"Fine. I'm glad," he responded sharply, angry now himself.

Brian picked up his machete and returned to work. What a prig, he thought, and it's just plain bad luck for the rest of us to be saddled with her type.

Min had a young Thai assistant who marched far at the rear of the party while others cleared the path. Besides watching for stragglers, this man carried a heavy load of vegetables on his back in an elongated basket supported by two straps tied in a thick band around his forehead. The group of tourists in front of the assistant were international in scope. In addition to the two Americans, there was a married Israeli couple and two robust German boys in their early twenties who had already paired off with two Italian girls about the same age. The only inexperienced hikers, other than Ellen, were the Italians who made up for their deficiencies with boundless enthusiasm in a desire to keep up with the boys.

Ellen's apparent aloofness, as they boarded the small truck in Chiang Mai early that morning, had caused Brian to sit with the young German boys. The age difference hardly mattered.

Their constant laughter was infectious and contributed to Brian's anticipation for the trek. The tourists had come into this remote area of Thailand to see an ethnic variety of native hill people in their own habitat before civilization from the growing urban population changed their village life forever. The truck, called a Bemo by the Asians, had plank-like metal seats facing each other. The vehicle had bumped and lurched from side to side, throwing the occupants against each other during the long ride over rough dirt roads before a drop-off point was reached at last. At the end of the trek the Bemo was scheduled to be waiting for the party some sixty miles away. Brian had glanced over at Ellen a few times while they had bounced around as rag dolls. She seemed so uncomfortable and out of place that he had avoided her while everyone unloaded their packs from the truck.

The column had now started to climb out of the bamboo forest higher into hill country. As the sun moved down to the peaks of the hills in front of them, Brian played an active role with the men in cutting a larger path through the last difficult section of the grove while the women stayed back. Soon, the group came out into a reasonably flat rice paddy divided by a series of raised earth mounds. Here the going became easier while the party walked carefully along the rims of the banks built as dikes to retain rain water for the rice crop.

It grew dark as the group began their final river crossing for the day. Min was exhorting them all to hurry in the fading light. The mud and silt at the bottom of the fast moving water was like quicksand in spots and everyone fought for decent footing. Brian joked with the four young people as they waded into dirty water churning up to their thighs. Ellen had fallen well back of the Israeli couple and was being accompanied by Min's assistant, a

kindly looking Thai with a tanned, moon-shaped face. There was
a loud splash. One of the Italian girls had slipped into a mudhole
and was stuck. The German boys dragged her out covered with
a plaster-coated brown goo. She yelped and screamed while the
boys cleaned her up by dousing her with handfuls of cold river
water. Ellen arrived on this scene and shook her head, smiling
in amusement.

Nightfall was upon them as the party formed up again on the
opposite side of the river. Min climbed up a dirt embankment so
that he was above his group. He had introduced himself to the
tourists at the start of the trek as a former Burmese Army officer, explaining that he had escaped the repressive Socialist government in Burma by hiking over the border into Thailand three
years earlier. Min's lean features were much sharper in contrast
than those of his assistant, his face more alert. He was dressed
in military-style fatigues and stood erect in front of his charges
as if he were about to address a squad of soldiers out on maneu-
vers. Min cupped his hands over his mouth.

"Listen up troops!" he cried. "We are going to have to stay
closer together. It will to be hard to see our way and we still have
two more hours of walking before reaching the village."

The tourists groaned in unison, bringing a smirk to Min's face.
Although his tone was commanding, they all realized his military
demeanor was partially an act. Nevertheless, Min appeared to
be a competent and knowledgeable leader.

"Yes, yes…I know you are tired," he continued, "but we must
get a move on. There are no more rivers or bamboo; however we
still have a forest to go through, so take the flashlights out of
your pack, adventure-lovers, and let's get started!"

With this order, the wiry tour leader jumped off the embankment and set off at a brisk pace on a new trail into the dense cluster of tall trees. Only half the people had brought flashlights and as they marched along, the trekkers resembled a huge disjointed glowworm snaking through the jungle. Ellen had no light and since everyone else had paired off again, she moved up close behind Brian to take advantage of his yellow beam bobbing out in front of them on the trail.

The night grew cool and Ellen felt stronger. Walking with the others under the black screen of thick tree branches, she became more aware of belonging to the group. The two Americans did not talk for a while, yet each was acutely conscious of the other as they traveled together in the quietness at the end of the column. Finally, Ellen broke the silence.

"Look, I'm sorry I snapped at you back there."

Brian knew the words came hard for her and he realized he was disturbed himself over her lack of ease with him.

"It's been a long day," he said. "We're all tired."

The narrow path wound through a forest of large, highly polished teak trees, effectively containing their conversation to the space between them while the rest of their party was strung out up the trail.

"You really like this sort of thing, don't you?" Ellen ventured. "The physical exertion, I mean."

"Yes, I suppose I do. I live in a small town not far from Eugene, Oregon. I'm a high school coach."

"Oh, a physical education teacher. Well, that explains it, then," Ellen declared.

Brian turned toward her in the darkness, unsure if he had heard a note of derision from this off-handed comment.

"Explains what? Is that meant as a put down?"

"My, you are touchy," she exclaimed, gaining more confidence somehow from his discomfort.

Brian said nothing while he pulled back a heavy growth of vines hanging down in their path, not warning her as he released them with a smack. Ellen chuckled lightly, catching the foliage with her arm as she moved past.

"What I meant was," she continued, "you are obviously a man who thrives on a lot of physical activity."

Her words were sharp, and hung in the air. Brian paused before answering her. He fought his rising temper, wondering why she was goading him in this way. Abruptly, he stopped and turned around to face her.

"Listen," he said, his voice filled with exasperation, "this trip into the bush is more than just a hike for me. It's an opportunity to see a simple culture that is still unspoiled."

"Ah, spoken as a true explorer," she laughed.

It was a nice laugh, he admitted to himself, like tinkling bells at Christmas time. Was she being sarcastic? Brian couldn't be sure. He pointed his flashlight directly at her. For the first time, he carefully examined Ellen illuminated against the darkness. He saw a slender, vivacious, determined-looking woman. Under the disheveled auburn hair, her keen, gray eyes were leveled at him. She gave him a tight smile which he interpreted as mocking.

Brian hesitated and then bored in, overreacting to her in a manner that was disconcerting even to him.

"I'm surprised you came on this trip at all," he said harshly, flinging the words at Ellen. "You are in lousy shape. I heard you puffing away this afternoon. I think you really have the wrong attitude for this trek. I'm sure the rest of us want it to be a unique experience. Why didn't you stay home in Boston, or wherever it is you come from?"

Brian turned away from her and hurried forward. It's time to back off, she thought, controlling her own temper. The man is probably bothered by the impression that I think of him as having a jock mentality.

They continued along the trail in silence while catching up to the others. Ellen thought she might have misjudged him; she was uncertain. She decided to answer his question.

"I'm here because I enjoy new experiences too," she said, pushing aside the trapped feelings she had actually felt earlier in the day. "I believe if you were to ask all eight members of our party you would get eight different reasons for coming on this trip."

Ellen knew she spoke evasively. She did not intend to justify herself to him, although her own motivations for the trip truthfully leaned toward a kind of internal escapism rather than a desire for cultural enrichment.

Brian did not respond to her.

"By the way, I'm not from Boston," she told him somewhat testily, "it's San Francisco."

"That figures—still an uptown girl." Brian groused over his shoulder dismissively.

They did not speak again. After another half-hour of gradual climbing, the group arrived at the crest of a hill where Min called a halt. Down below the hill the tourists saw plumes of sparks flying skyward from a large bonfire centered in a forest clearing. A ring of thatched dwellings on stilts stood on one side of the fire.

"Folks, this is the village of the Yellow Lahu people," Min announced. "You are only the second party to visit this village. You will all be placed in one large hut. As we come into the village, please arrange yourselves and your gear against the two longest walls, four on each side, opposite one another. This way the Yellow Lahu can receive and serve you from the ends of the room."

As the party entered the village, the children came out to meet them first. Shy, they ran in all directions before escorting the tourists to a rectangular bungalow in the center of the village. The Israeli couple held back, fascinated by the clothes of the Yellow Lahu. Both men and women of this tribe wore black tunics with silver buttons stitched in rows down the front. The men had on short, baggy pants which ended at their knees, while the women wore long black skirts of rough cotton with the edges trimmed in colorful strips of yellow and red cloth.

Climbing the stairs into the largest hut, the group found that mats had been placed for them over bamboo slats tied in flat strips. This offered some protection from the drafty wooden floor planks underneath, built seven feet above the ground. Ellen pinched her nose at the whiffs of stench rising from under the floor. Animal waste and garbage were in evidence under every hut. The sleeping arrangements unsettled Ellen further. The German boys with their Italian girlfriends had immediately rushed in and thrown their gear down together along one wall. Laughing and shoving each other playfully with uninhibited excitement, the boys joked with the girls about how their current sleeping positions could be modified again during the night. On the opposite side of the hut, the Israeli couple smiled at the young people and, laying down their packs, began to converse quietly. The two remaining side-by-side mats were left for the Americans. Ellen wanted a corner off by herself for some privacy. None was available.

Brian sensed her discomfort. Keeping his voice low, he said, "It looks as though we're going to be thrown together in one way or another in the days ahead whether we like it or not. I suggest some kind of truce. I know we don't suit each other, but we'll just have to make the best of our situation and at least try to be civil. Otherwise, the trip will be miserable for us and everyone else."

"Well, no one seems to be paying much attention to us, anyway," she said, frowning. Ellen knew he was right but she felt stubborn nonetheless.

"Maybe not yet, but they will if the bad feeling between us grows. We are too close a group. So what do you say? My name is Brian," he said holding out his hand.

"All right," she sighed with resignation, "mine is Ellen."

She held out her small hand briefly and then sat down on her bed roll.

"Good," Brian said simply, crouching down and arranging his bed roll alongside her own. He nodded at the Israelis and struck up a conversation with them.

Ellen felt disoriented and the earlier concerns of being completely out of her element had returned. Her usual defenses for controlling, or at least mollifying, distasteful situations were of no use to her here.

The men of the tribe filed into the room and sat down cross-legged in front of their guests. Some of the women and children, their faces expectant, followed behind carrying food. Min and his assistant helped distribute hot portions of rice, a little chicken, parsley, onions and peanuts mixed in wooden bowls. The party was then served tea. As the Westerners began to eat, a sea of weathered, inquisitive faces watched every move with intense interest. Their black, almond-shaped eyes glittered above rows of silver buttons in the flickering candlelight.

"Do you get the feeling we are regarded as alien beings from another planet?" Brian whispered to Ellen, in an attempt to be companionable.

She looked over at him while he ate ravenously. The joyful grin on Brian's open features was infectious, even disarming to her. He reminded Ellen of her brother as a small boy.

"We are from another world," she agreed.

More people entered the large room, many holding smoking pipes in their hands, bringing a pungent scent into the confined space. As the meal drew to a close, Min's voice cut through the smoky haze.

"Some of you may recognize the smell of opium," he announced. "These people regularly smoke opium, especially after meals and as a form of hospitality. This custom is a habit with many other Burmese who have settled in the hills of Northern Thailand. Burma was not their original home. Centuries ago, the ancestors of these hill people journeyed from Tibet and China down through the province of Yunan into Burma."

"But why did they leave Burma to come here?" the Israeli man asked Min.

"For the same reason I did, to escape from a repressive government. The Burmese government wants the army to break up the hill tribes in Burma. They are less tolerant than Thailand when it comes to making and trading in drugs," Min said.

"Is there regular drug trading going on here?" Brian asked their tour guide.

"Yes, and I will explain more about this later. Many of the poppy fields we will see on this trip are for the individual tribe's own use—in making opium from their plants. Almost everyone smokes some opium," Min went on, "and those of you who wish, can participate in other villages. Because we have arrived behind schedule tonight, the Yellow Lahu are now ready to dance for you."

The group filed outside to the large bonfire still crackling at the edge of the village. The native men at once formed a circle and began a tribal dance, their feet shuffling slowly in a sidestep motion. While the men twisted rightward around the fire, the women joined hands and danced to the left just behind them.

The women chanted in low, resonant tones to a mournful tune played by a tribal musician on a wooden flute. Min quietly explained that the honor of providing music for the dance was reserved solely for this medicine man of the village. His influence with nature went far beyond curative powers. Min said the role of a holy man caused the tribe to treat him with more respect than even the chief because of his influence with the spirits of good and evil. The eerie patterns of notes chosen and shaped by the flute player subtly created a kind of hypnotic trance among the dancers who felt the vibrations came from a higher source. The ghost-like figures moved in cadence to this music, absorbing their connection to ancient tribal spirits through the dance.

The massive trees which stood around the village, just outside the firelight, girdled the tourists in their embrace. Under the banded stars of a brilliant white Milky Way, Ellen found herself captured in this primeval scene. After a while, the chief indicated the outsiders would be welcome to join in the dancing. Tentatively, Brian reached for Ellen's hand as the tourists clasped hands with the Yellow Lahu and awkwardly tried to imitate the native dance steps. Inhibitions were put aside and soon their movements became more natural with encouragement from the tribal dancers.

As the dancing progressed, Ellen felt a strange sensation of harmony and peace come over her. The two Americans beheld each other, at first self-consciously, then trusting to the enchantment they were experiencing together they moved in a circle around the fire. In this moment, each saw the other in a different light than before. Each saw a graceful tranquility in the other which blended with what they both felt as the dance consumed them. The black figures of the Yellow Lahu whirled, holding the hands of the tourists, carrying them into a mystical transmigration.

At last the rite ended. Brian and Ellen unconsciously held hands for a moment longer before releasing.

"That was wonderful," he said softly, keenly aware of Ellen beside him.

"Like magic," she answered, a wan smile on her face.

Everyone then applauded and slowly left the circle of flickering light for their respective dwellings.

"Tired?" Brian asked as he walked back with her.

"Yes—very," she sighed quietly.

They followed the others inside the large bungalow and it was not long before the weary party fell sleep. Ellen listened to their discordant snoring. These noises, coupled with the inert presence of the stranger sleeping next to her, kept Ellen awake despite her fatigue. She felt uncomfortable lying beside Brian in such incongruent circumstances. Who was this person with whom she had so little in common? She tried to sort out the extraordinary events of the day. It was odd being thrown into an environment so different from her own life where she had time to plan and make suitable adjustments to situations. The chill on her back from the cold floor caused her to shiver. A gecko scampered across the ceiling emitting a peculiar clacking noise. She heard pigs grunting under the bungalow, searching for edible waste. From a distance, there was an occasional gonging sound from the pear-shaped bells attached to the necks of water buffalo wandering near the village. At last, Ellen's fatigue took her into sleep.

Shortly after dawn, most of the men in the village were already on their way to nearby fields down the mountainside.

Ellen awoke drowsily to Min's exhortations for everyone to get up and pack their gear. She felt as if she had just gone to sleep. Sitting up stiffly, she accepted the hot tea, hard boiled eggs and wedges of bread that were being passed around to her companions. When breakfast was finished, everyone assembled outside and said goodbye to the local women who stood by grinning toothlessly at the tourists. The village had changed for Ellen in the starkness of daylight. It now looked rather squalid to her.

Brian had been in conversation with the Israelis and he came over to her.

"Are your muscles sore today?" He inquired with jaunty humor.

"What muscles?" Ellen said, frowning at him. Thinking cynically, she wondered if he was being solicitous to the point of condescension. The exertions from yesterday had thrown her out of kilter this morning. It had been a bad night on the cold, hard floor with her body aching all over and wearing dirty clothes, stiff from dried sweat.

She was having trouble with her backpack. Brian stepped behind her and helped adjust the straps on the small canvas pack until it fit snugly between her shoulder blades.

"Thanks, that's better," she said, embarrassed, keenly aware that no one else appeared to need any help.

The party set off for a strenuous day of many river crossings as they hiked down into steaming valleys and then up into hill country that was higher than the previous day. While the tourists passed near other small villages, their guide showed them cultivated poppy fields.

"Opium flowers," Min announced, pointing to plots of ground covered by leafy plant stalks topped with blooms of various colors.

"Look at these plants of the poppy family," Min said. "Red, pink, purple and white. The white flower plants have a false reputation for making the best opium. Those who work these fields know that color has no bearing on either the quality or quantity of production," he explained further.

The guide bent down and with a sharp knife he slit a pod capsule within the folds of a poppy bloom. After extracting a few seeds, Min opened the capsule wider and carried it around to show each member of the group.

"It is the milky juice, dried and hardened, from these unripened seed pods which make opium, not the seeds themselves," Min went on.

Not long after his illustrations with the opium plant, Min led the party near a sparse settlement of hill people. They were very poor. Dressed in shabby black and red garments, their bodies were covered with dirt. Most were emaciated.

"Here are a few Akhu people—this is what too much opium can do," Min said severely. "They have become useless outcasts from larger tribes of Akhu. The men here smoke opium day and night. They do no work. They live in a dream world. They are hopeless addicts and so their women must weave many mats and baskets to sell to other villagers in order to feed their children.

The children looked sick and lifeless to the tourists.

"What happened to them? How did all this start?" the group asked.

"An addict does not smoke opium for hospitality anymore," Min continued. "The tranquilizer we call 'The Lady of Sleep' has cast her spell on these Akhu who once lived in other villages. These addicts come here to dream together because their Akhu tribes do not want them."

"Do the women smoke much opium?" one of the Italian girls inquired.

"Usually, no—or at least very little," Min answered. "This is because someone must care for the children. Opium smoking begins for the first time with young people as a social ceremony, but opium also relieves pain and hunger. The result is some of the poor tribes use it too much."

"Why doesn't the government do something?" Ellen exclaimed.

"The Thai government does not want internal rebellions to develop in this border country by restricting opium harvesting," Min explained patiently. "They have enough political problems with unfriendly neighbors in Burma, Cambodia, Laos and Vietnam without bringing about additional unrest at home."

"Plus, not wanting to interrupt a lucrative drug trade in Bangkok, I'll bet," chimed in one of German boys.

"Who am I to say?" Min responded evasively. "Yet the government does hold out the promise of citizenship, schools, and food if the Burmese hill people show proper respect for Thai laws."

"I think what opium has done to these people is awful. Just look at these poor children!" Ellen cried.

"True, it is not good," Min said. "These addicts do not care anymore about the realities of this world, but I will leave them some of our rice."

Min spoke rapidly to his assistant who gave some of the stores he was carrying to an Akhu woman. She bowed to the tourists in gratitude.

As the group moved on, Ellen found herself very disturbed by the lethargic drug addicts she had seen. To some extent, it spoiled the sense of attachment she had begun to feel with the festive Yellow Lahu the night before. After the Akhu village was out of sight, Brian came up beside her.

"And, how do you cope with the realities of this world?" he asked, picking up on Min's comments about the effects of opium. Brian's manner sounded rather callous to her after what they had witnessed with the Akhu.

"Not with drugs, I can assure you!"

"I'm sure you don't. In fact you seem like a highly disciplined and organized woman to me—away from here, of course," he said, teasing her.

"Do I really appear to be that much of a misfit?" Ellen asked defiantly, still upset.

Brian shook his head. He caught her mood finally and was at once sorry for his remarks.

"No, you're wrong, I didn't mean it that way, Ellen. Sure, I was kidding you some, but you're doing fine." When she didn't answer, he went on. "I didn't like what we saw either, but these people have their own customs and live the way they want. After all, we are the outsiders."

"Oh, I see," she said bitterly, "and so we should not try to do anything about the social ills of others in the world."

"Dammit, Ellen, we have enough social problems in our own country to worry about without interfering with other cultures," he answered her crisply.

"Well, Brian, I guess that indicates how unlike we are," she said slowly.

They spoke no more for a while. Ellen walked along with her eyes downcast. This bothered Brian and he didn't understand why. He wanted to straighten out what he said to her on a personal level before the conversation had turned to drugs.

"How could you believe that I think you're a misfit here after watching you dance last night," he said.

She looked up at Brian and measured him, realizing that he was sincere and trying to make amends. She appreciated men who said what was on their minds, but she was used to subtle men, some of whom had hidden agendas. It was the blunt directness of this man which unnerved her.

"I'm sure on your home turf you are probably very accomplished," Brian added with conviction, smiling at her. "I wouldn't want to be the one who got in your way."

"Oh, I'm not all that formidable, even for an uptown girl," she said reproachfully with a short laugh, arching an eyebrow at him.

The tension between them eased. With Brian's coaxing she began telling him about her architectural work and the discrimination she felt by simply being female. She explained how this had made her work harder to achieve her goals.

"And how about your life?" she asked him abruptly.

"Not much to tell, really. I had a sporting goods store for a while. It failed because of some rash business decisions on my part. I moved to a smaller community where the basic values of day-to-day living are appreciated. Because I had a good athletic record in school and loved working with kids, I got into coaching. There are no long-range goals in my life. I take each day as it comes."

Brian stopped talking. He wondered about his willingness to reveal the private aspects of his life to her.

The party traversed into a wide valley between two hump-backed mountains allowing for a flat, straight approach toward a river a quarter mile away. Min set a comfortable pace for his charges so they could relax and enjoy the surroundings. His assistant threaded his way forward to the guide to talk, leaving the Americans virtually alone.

Ellen decided that her assumptions about Brian had been wrong. In the beginning, she thought he was insensitive and egocentric. His large physical presence and abrupt manner initially misled her into believing he was one-dimensional. It was refreshing to find a man without artifice or self-deception. However, she didn't like his impulsiveness. She came to the conclusion he was a lonely man, contained within himself.

"If we consider life as a department store, I guess you would put sports in the toy section?" Brian asked out of the blue.

Ellen burst out laughing, restraining herself only after she saw the serious look on his face.

"Why should I think that! You have a false impression of me. I don't denigrate sports. Helping kids is a fine profession," she answered him. When he didn't respond she went on: "Look, each person shapes their own destiny and in the end you are what you want to be."

"And are you where you want to be in San Francisco?"

"Oh, I suppose so," Ellen said vaguely. "I did what I set out to do. I've gained respect for my work and all…"

Brian saw that her eyes were clouded. The Americans had lagged behind the rest of the company who were now unloading their packs by a quiet bend of the river. The water, shimmering in the midafternoon sun, meandered a slow course across the delta below the mountains. It was a gentle, peaceful setting.

"Are you involved with someone at home?" He said unexpectedly.

Ellen flushed. She was both annoyed and put off-balance by his question and it took her a moment to recover.

"No, not anymore," she said finally, thinking of the times her trust had been misplaced and the emptiness which followed.

"I have no right to pry," he said with chagrin.

"It's all right." Ellen said, still struggling with herself. She fixed her eyes on him. "What about you?"

"I've struck out in that area, I'm afraid," he said with a forced casualness that belied his feelings. "As you may have noticed, I have a bad habit of saying exactly what is on my mind, and not always tactfully, I've been told. I just scare women off—or at least the ones I thought I cared about."

Ellen regarded him intently, respecting his candor.

"Maybe you are too overbearing for the faint-hearted," she smiled enigmatically, her eyes full of mischief.

"Is that how you see me?" Brian said seriously.

"Oh, well…maybe a little," Ellen bantered.

Brian was taken by her playfulness. Just when he thought he was beginning to understand her, she surprised him. He wanted to know more.

"Have you ever thought the person who loves the most is also the most defenseless in any relationship?" he asked.

"Do you really believe that nonsense?" Ellen fired back, her smile gone. "Loving makes you vulnerable—not defenseless."

"I've considered there is usually one who loves and one who allows himself to be loved," he said.

"And which one are you?" she asked, not agreeing with his premise, but curious nonetheless.

"Truthfully, I think I've gone both ways with women. I don't know on which side I belong in this formula."

Brian had struck a responsive cord within her, and Ellen's reaction was explosive.

"That's because there should be no side to that dumb formula. Don't you know real love must be given and received equally?"

"Isn't one person always more vulnerable?" Brian persisted.

"Not if both are giving one-hundred percent of themselves to make the relationship survive. Not if there is total commitment..." He saw she could not go on. Ellen's hands trembled and she shoved them down into her pockets out of sight.

"I can't argue with that," he said quietly. "I'm sure you must have given a hundred percent."

"I thought so at the time," she told him with a finality that effectively ended the conversation.

Walking next to Ellen as they approached the river, Brian thought of how he had initially been put off by this assertive woman, wanting to dislike her. She was not his type. He had avoided high-strung, intellectual women, not because they were hard to dominate—he didn't want to control anybody—but because he didn't understand them. He admitted to himself she had a great deal to give to a man who cared enough and was able to meet her challenges. That man would have to be someone very different from himself. There would be too much misunderstanding and conflict between them, he speculated.

Everyone assembled at the river's edge, and Min crawled up on top of a large boulder where he ceremoniously addressed the tourists.

"Troops, I have a surprise for you," he said grandly, folding his arms across his chest for effect. For all his good nature, Min was still an army man.

"The village on top of this hill behind me is the home of the Lisu tribe where we will stay the night. This means you may have the next couple of hours taking a bath here, cleaning and drying your clothes and resting in the sun while I help the Lisu prepare for dinner."

This announcement was immediately met with a chorus of delight by the group. Min waved his hand goodbye, jumped off the rock and with his assistant, set off up the hill.

The Italian and German tourists rapidly stripped off their clothes and flinging garments in all directions, leaped together into the cool water. The Israeli man and his wife decided to move a little further upstream, not out of embarrassment but to avoid being splashed by the young people who were thrashing around each other, whooping loudly. Everyone had been issued a small bar of bio-degradable soap, and the four people in the water began scrubbing off grime from their skins while jumping up and down from the cold.

Ellen and Brian grinned at those in the river and then surveyed each other as to who would be next. He saw that she was uncertain.

"I'm sure there are more secluded places up the river for the less daring," he teased, raising his eyebrows at her.

"Oh, it's too shallow up there and besides, modesty is not for the practical," she answered resolutely, pulling off her jeans.

In a gallant fashion, which she appreciated, Brian turned his back on Ellen and began undressing. He was surprised and strangely pleased that he had misjudged yet another aspect of her character. After removing her clothes, she skipped into the water to join the Italian girls. Brian finished taking off his boots and, standing up, he looked toward Ellen.

As he watched her wading out into the river, Brian unconsciously held his breath. The pretty Italians cavorting in the nude around Ellen did not exist for him. He was struck by Ellen's delicately proportioned figure and her graceful movements in the water. He tried to look away and failed. Brian saw her pause and he thought she would turn and catch him staring at her, but Ellen bent low to the current running against her legs and began to bathe. For a moment more he watched how the liquid from her cupped hands flowed over the curves of her supple body, the glazed wetness accentuating the elegance of her lines all the more. Letting his breath out slowly, Brian tried to collect himself and realized he simply could not bathe with her. Forcing himself to look away, he left the deeper pool and moved in the direction of the Israeli man washing near his wife.

Brian chatted with the couple awhile, and the Israeli woman commented that she thought it was nice he seemed to be getting on so well with the other single American in their party. Brian nodded politely, knowing the woman was curious why he was not bathing with Ellen. Eventually, the cold water drove everyone out. The tourists put on their underwear and spread the rest of their clothes out on rocks while they enjoyed the luxury of a slow dry-off in the sun. Ellen left the young people and came along the river toward Brian who was lying on a slab of rock by himself.

"Does the intrepid—rather shy adventurer—want any company?" Ellen said lightly.

"Absolutely," he said, glad that she had sought him out.

Sitting down next to him, she folded her legs sideways and started humming softly while brushing out her thick hair with a small hand towel.

"You remind me of one of those water nymphs I used to see on the old Shasta bottles," he said, trying to be casual. He found this easier if he avoided looking directly at her.

Ellen wrinkled her nose at him without answering as she examined his rugged features. Despite the appearance of an easy familiarity, each was aware of the other's underlying self-consciousness.

"Might I say, as a child of nature, you appear very fit and ready to go anywhere—except back to civilization," he said.

"Funny you should mention that," she said with an air of detachment. "It's wonderful to feel so free with no decisions to make and no stress of responsibility. You know what I mean?"

"My dear," Brian pronounced gravely, "by the authority vested in me, I set you free from the chains that bind you."

Leaning toward her, Brian traced a cross on Ellen's forehead with two fingers in mock benediction.

"And I should have faith in—you!" she smiled.

"Oh, yeah, otherwise it won't work. I give you permission," he laughed.

"I'm so grateful," Ellen said, backhanding a spray of water at his face from her wet hair.

While their clothes dried, they lay back against the warm rock and talked about inconsequential things. Both discovered that at unexpected moments when they were together in this way, without tension, their contrasting natures complemented each other in a fashion that neither could define. Without really being aware of this process, the scenes Brian and Ellen witnessed in the hills took on added significance as well. At the same time, because this affinity was new to them, it was also bound up in emotional conflict. While being drawn together, they fought within themselves to retain their individuality as a refuge in this strange country among people who believed in supernatural powers.

A cool breeze sent ripples across the water, while a storm was building westward over the mountains in the direction of Burma. Everyone got dressed. Soon Min returned, and the party reluctantly gathered their belongings and started up the steep hill to the Lisu village.

The natives of the colorful Lisu tribe met the tourists at the top. Like the Yellow Lahu and Akhu, the Lisu wore black, but added wide bands of red, yellow and violet strips of cloth to their vests, pants and skirts. These costumes were set off by beaded skull caps with tassels hanging down in back. Min led them into the largest thatched dwelling in the village. The group sat down and while an elderly Lisu woman served tea, Min decided this was an appropriate time for an explanation of the beliefs and cultural differences between Thailand's various hill tribes.

"These primitive tribes have a religion called animism," Min began. "I have heard that this was once the belief of all ancient people around the world. It is a belief that spirits inhabit both living and non-living things. Each tribe has a medicine man serving as a high priest who is able to converse with these spirits for the benefit of the tribe."

"So, they don't worship a single God?" one of the Italians inquired.

"Not really," Min answered, "but the sun is an all-powerful spirit. You must understand the hill tribes worship their surroundings. If anything of nature is destroyed or not treated with respect, a spirit could be offended and a penalty for the tribe might follow, such as a poor crop of rice. If the gods are angry and cause hardship the medicine man is blamed for a lack of communication. He does not have an easy life."

"But isn't most of Thailand, Buddhist?" the Israeli man spoke up.

"Yes, that is true," Min answered. "Even though animism was here first, Buddhists also believe soul-spirits exist everywhere. This makes the two belief systems compatible in our country. However, while all the tribes are animists, there are distinct differences between them that I should tell you about."

Min then explained that the Yellow Lahu of the previous day had a primary desire for freedom of thought and expression, while the Akhu people desired continuity with their ancestors above all else. He gave the tourists examples of other tribal distinctions such as the Karen, whose major goal in life was to blend well into their environment. Min ended these comparisons with the Lisu.

"Since we are now with the Lisu, be aware that if one can speak Lisu they can communicate with all other tribes. There is a common understanding of the Lisu language. The reason for this is that the Lisu are the trading merchants in opium for all other tribes. Some tribes do not have enough land to cultivate much opium. The Lisu grow no opium themselves so they will not be in competition with their customers. They are prosperous because all members of their tribe participate equally in the opium profits, not only the leaders.

"But why the Lisu?" the group all asked at once.

"Because, of all the hill people, they have the greatest desire to be good middlemen in business and to settle disputes between tribes," Min said, basking in the rapt attention he was receiving from his group. "The Lisu do not have to farm much. Other tribes come to barter pigs, chickens, vegetables, and rice for opium. Lisu men and women have money and use it wisely. Lisu girls who are hard-working bring a much higher price in a marriage contract than the lazy ones in this commercial village," he added.

Brian turned to Ellen and under his breath said, "As a female slave to the work ethic, I imagine you would come rather high?"

"Certainly," she replied at once. "And please notice that no mention is made of the potentially lazy husbands in this tribal arrangement."

Dinner that night in the Lisu village was unexpectedly good, with Min helping the cooks prepare chicken and rice mixed with spinach in a huge pot. Following the tasty meal, the guide introduced a full-blooded Chinese man, stooped with age and totally bald.

"This fellow is called the professor of opium," Min declared. "Originally, he was a teacher in Shanghai who had to escape during Mao's cultural revolution when the intellectuals were purged in Red China. Eventually, he was able to cross into Thailand and has lived in contented obscurity with the Lisu for a long time. The professor would be glad to instruct you in the art of opium smoking since he speaks a number of languages. There will be a small charge for the opium each of you use because with the Lisu, nothing is free."

The proceedings especially interested the German boys who watched intently as the old Chinese brought out a used sardine can and a cloth-covered headrest. Inside the tin was a small smoking pipe, a slender metal spoon pointed at the end, and a white cube of opium. Setting a candle in front of his materials, the teacher indicated that his guests should move in closer.

"Ladies and gentleman," he began, "I shall introduce the subject of opium to you by first defining the origins of the plant you have seen in the hills around us. Thousands of years ago opium existed in Mesopotamia and Persia. In the classical period of Greece, opium expanded into the Mediterranean. Knowledge of the drug spread into Europe from Rome, and by the seventh century it had arrived in Asia through India. In my own country of China, opium has been available for only three hundred years, although it has acquired a bad reputation there because of the Opium Wars. There was a time in China when it was called 'the Curse of the Poppy.' This was due to excessive abuse that was made worse from illegal smuggling by foreign traders."

"Opium can be beneficial or a harsh taskmaster," the teacher remarked with an impassive expression, his eyes hooded. "If chemically separated, it will produce the narcotics you know as morphine, codeine and heroin. Please do not concern yourselves tonight about bad reactions. Here we have just the basic substance of pure opium, and I will carefully measure the dosages. Now I will illustrate to you the proper way to use opium," the Chinese man said, regarding each of the tourists.

Holding the opium cake in his hand, he announced, "What you see here is opium that has already been prepared for smoking by prolonged boiling in water. The impurities have then been removed through evaporation to give it the consistency of putty."

Taking a pinch of opium and placing it at the end of his stylet, the man gradually heated the spoon over the candle flame until a small ball of roasted opium was formed to his satisfaction.

"As you will observe," the teacher went on, "I am now gently pushing the heated opium into my pipe for a smoke."

After doing so, the old man lay down on his side with his head resting on the hard pillow for maximum results. He inhaled deeply for a few minutes and then rose to a sitting position again.

"Once reaching the lungs, the effects are immediate," he said. "However, notice the opium is rapidly used up and a new dose must be added and held over the flame to maintain heat for prolonged smoking. The formalities are over. Who is ready for the first smoke?"

"I hope you all enjoyed the professor's demonstration," Min said. "As I told you, opium smoking is sociable in moderation. It is the way all hill tribes show hospitality," he said encouragingly.

"How does opium affect one?" asked the Israeli woman. She and Ellen still had the pathetic Akhu addicts on their minds.

"A few puffs only and you will feel very calm and relaxed. You are released from the cares of the world and you will sleep better, too," the Chinese man answered.

Everyone except Ellen and the Israeli woman decided to smoke a little opium. The Lisu brought in more pipes for the ritual while the teacher assisted anyone who wanted help. Brian and the Israeli man took a short smoke and passed their pipes to the German boys who waited to be last because they wanted to feel the effects of a longer smoke.

Brian rejoined Ellen at the far end of the room where she was sitting on the floor. He saw a sour look on her face.

"I know the whole idea of drugs disturbs you," he said, in an attempt to diffuse her annoyance, "but this tribe seems to know how to handle it, don't you think?"

Ellen, turned away from him, not answering. She wrapped her arms around her knees. To Brian, her slim body appeared as a tightly wound ball, resistant to his presence. Frustrated, he continued to talk.

"And, as long as it's not overdone, the drug can lift the hill people out of their hard lives for a while."

"That's just the point, don't you see?" Ellen broke in, exasperated. "For whatever reason, it is overdone everywhere. You know these people ship the stuff to other locations for the international drug trade," she scolded. "How can you excuse this? We have a worldwide epidemic of drug addiction by people who want to escape from reality instead of facing life with a clear mind."

Brian grew agitated by the change in her disposition when everyone else in their group was having a good time.

"Oh, come on, Ellen," he said in disgust. "We've been over this ground before. Can't you keep the traditions of these people in proper perspective without bringing in the ills of the rest of the world? Dammit, why are you so uptight about everything?"

"And why are you so casual about things that really matter?" she said angrily. "Are you so unconcerned about this issue that you wouldn't care if the kids you coach were strung out on drugs?"

Brian was stung by this remark and hurt that it came from her after their day at the river. He felt like striking back hard at her.

"Of course not, and you know that's an unfair comparison! Ellen, I've come to the conclusion that you could stand to have a little euphoria in your life. It might make you more fun to be around."

"Thanks for that, Brian," she said coldly.

Later that night it grew unusually chilly as a severe rainstorm blew in and lashed the thatched roofs of the village. The single blanket issued to each member of the party was not enough. Members of the group began to share their blankets and huddle close together on the drafty floor. Brian rolled over and was awakened by Ellen's uncontrollable shivering.

"Look, Ellen," he whispered, "this is stupid, slide over next to me for warmth and let's use both our blankets."

Both of them had too much pride to be the first to apologize so soon after their quarrel. Cautiously, Ellen moved nearer to Brian without acknowledging how much she needed his warmth. As she shifted her position, Brian was aroused by the soft contours of her body coming against him. His blood rose and he felt a tingling in his ears. There was no provocation on her part—he knew Ellen only sought warmth—yet he wished she would unbend a little. Brian did not intend to be conciliatory because he was still miffed with her, nonetheless his arm went around her shoulders naturally, with no conscious will on his part. Ellen stiffened.

"Oh, come on, you're freezing," he said.

The resonance of Brian's voice and his body warmth was comforting, but she would not release the hold on herself.

"Is that better?" he asked, feeling unsettled by her closeness.

"Yes, it is warmer," she acknowledged matter-of-factly from the dark void between them, still remote and unwilling to give up the need for her own space.

"You wouldn't be much good to us with pneumonia," he said in a forced tone. When she did not respond, he gave up. Soon her shaking ceased but he made no further attempt to draw her closer.

After a while, Ellen heard Brian's regular breathing again as the rain-filled wind beat against the roof. God, he can sleep through anything, she thought. As usual, it was difficult to quiet her restless mind and go to sleep, all the more so since she was now lying next to him. She tried to unravel her emotions about the man beside her. Ellen's normal confidence in knowing herself had weakened in the last few days. Was it due to Brian himself, or her displacement in this exotic setting where two strangers from the same country had been thrown together? Would he have made any impression on her if this were San Francisco? Perhaps not, she didn't know. The telescoping of time during the trek made such comparisons difficult. All she knew was that Brian both attracted and caused her to resist him, depending upon the circumstances. His self-assurance calmed her in some situations and infuriated her in others. They approached life differently. Their arguments about drug use was a prime example. Brian's attitude could indicate he lacked the same degree of conscience as herself, or was she over-reaching?

Despite her misgivings, Ellen accepted the fact there was a growing expectancy within her about this man and she recognized the danger signals produced by these feelings. She did not trust herself. They clashed too much with their opinions. It was prudent to erect a protective shield against being hurt. She had already revealed too much of herself. She must be careful. As the hour grew late, Ellen fell into a troubled slumber.

Just after dawn, Brian awoke to find Ellen turned sideways against him, cradled by his arm. Her head nestled comfortably on his shoulder. Strands of hair were in disarray around her cheek and he carefully lifted them back. He felt a profound contentment as he looked down on her, wishing he could hold back the day. The storm had passed, bringing a freshness to the air in the village. He heard hens clucking outside and further away a rooster was crowing. Watching Ellen's tranquil state gave him a feeling that there was an impenetrable mystery about her he could not fathom but which curiously made him more alive. She fascinated and disturbed him.

She stirred beside him, partially opening her eyes still heavy from sleep. For an instant she smiled faintly up at him and there was the ageless understanding between a man and woman who are connected. The moment passed quickly as her eyes cleared. Brian saw her face become drawn and on guard. Then, self-consciously, she moved away from him, believing the others might misconstrue their sleeping arrangements.

Brian's contentment evaporated as he saw her frigid mantle unfold. While the others were rising, he busied himself with his kit and rolling up their blankets. He handed Ellen her blanket with an exaggerated arm motion.

"The two blankets worked well, didn't they?" he said. His feeble attempt at conversation had a hollow ring.

"Yes, it was...good. Thank you. I'm afraid I don't do very well when it's cold," she answered him passively, still tired from lack of sleep.

While Ellen collected her gear in a methodical manner, Brian had the impression an emotional trap door was closing in his face.

Hell, she's actually apologizing for needing me last night, he thought. Brian came to a decision. This is going to stop right now, he resolved. My first impression of her was right. We were a mismatch from the beginning. I'm going to keep away from her altogether for the rest of the trip. She won't ruin the trek for me. Immediately, he began planning how he would hike with other people. For that matter, he told himself, he could enjoy the time remaining by just hiking alone. He felt better already.

Soon a breakfast of tea, bread and jam was served with hardboiled eggs. Ellen was with the Israeli couple, studiously avoiding making eye contact with him. Good, Brian thought, I'll join the young people. As they finished, Min came into the room and outlined his plans for the day.

"Folks, we have some work ahead of us," he began cheerfully. "The good news is, it will not be as cold tonight in our last camp with the Red Lahu tribe. They live at a lower altitude. Tomorrow, we will have a long but easy walk out to the road junction where our Bemo is to meet us for the return to Chiang Mai by evening."

While Min went back to the kitchen to return the tribe's blankets and finish packing their lunch, the party went outside. Ellen and the women of the group played a game of betel nuts with the Lisu children, rolling the hard, perfectly rounded nuts down a smooth dirt strip to strike a set of three wooden pegs stuck in the ground. They were no match for the youngsters who shrieked with delight at each victory. Finally, the party bid their farewells to the Lisu people and followed Min off the top of the hill on a gradually descending path, skirting the barrier of a high mountain immediately to the west. The village of traders rapidly disappeared from view.

Brian had positioned himself away from Ellen at the front of the line among the better hikers. Within a few hours the climb into a lower range of mountains became much harder with the rising and falling terrain. Just before the intended lunch break, the group passed a few Shan tribesmen. These men were an ugly lot in dirty loin cloths, their upper torsos and faces tattooed with black marks of manhood. Each man carried over his shoulder a long bamboo pole sharpened at one end. The Shan leered directly at the Western women while keeping their distance off to the side of the trail.

"Not friendly," Min cried, trying unsuccessfully to mask his concern, "we keep going."

An hour later, during lunch, two Shan were seen on a low ridge behind the party. They sat on their haunches and watched the tourists eating. Min grew more anxious and urged his group to finish up so they could get started. Had he known about the possibility of Shan scouts in this area, he would have taken a different route. There were Shan clans who were hospitable, but many were more aggressive and warlike than the other tribes. The guide could not alarm his group by telling them that some Shan tribes had the reputation of being thieves. Min remembered a party of tourists he had led last year down the Kok River border country, dividing Laos from Thailand. Shan bandits had pulled out from the Laotian shoreline into the center of the river and rammed their narrow metal boat, boarded and stole everyone's valuables. He had lost a fine watch to these robbers. It could have been worse.

Occasionally, there were stories of physical abuse and killings by the Shan which the Thai guides tried to suppress. If this information became generally known, it would hurt the tourist trade.

The humidity had increased dramatically in the early afternoon as the party hiked over the last crest of an outcropping of hills adjacent to the Pai River, an Eastern tributary of the giant Salween in Burma. The Pai had carved out a shallow ravine which the tourists had to hike through. Climbing down slowly, the party observed the forests of teak and ironwood thinning out as they entered a valley. The lower elevations brought back the troublesome bamboo and thick brush. Cutting their way through clumps of vines, the group was once again strung out, with Brian and the German boys up front clearing a better pathway with their machetes. Deciding to take a break, Brian stretched and removed his drenched shirt, stuffing it into his backpack. He noticed Min's assistant idly walking nearby rather than in his usual place at the end of the line. Suddenly, he thought of Ellen's safety. He turned around and looked at the small hill in back of them. His senses now alert, Brian left his place and threaded his way past those behind him until he reached the Israeli couple at the rear. Leaning on their walking sticks, they told him between gulps of water they had not seen Ellen for ten, maybe fifteen minutes. They said a colorful parrot had flown over Ellen's head and she wanted to investigate the spot where it landed. Brian saw that the man and his wife were more focused on how tired they were than on Ellen. There was a queer tugging sensation in the pit of his stomach.

Brian dropped his pack and began to run, driving his legs like pistons down the path and back up the hill that everyone had passed over except Ellen. The trail made a dog-leg to his right, out of sight from the rest of the party. Brian slipped on the loose rock along the edge of the slope and kept going. He zigzagged upwards through a narrow passage of heavy foliage near the summit. Frantically, he scrambled forward, still not seeing her anywhere. The footing was poor and Brian staggered against a clump of sharp bamboo, tearing a gash across his right knee. Feeling no pain, he plunged along to the crest of the hill where at last he had a clear view of the valley the party had passed through.

Brian scanned the trail as it descended down into a series of switchbacks before blending with the valley floor. Then he saw her. An icy chill crawled up his spine. Ellen was alone in heavy undergrowth, her attention centered on a brightly-hued parrot in a thicket of rosewood branches. She stood off the path, oblivious of everything but the beautiful olive-green bird with a blue-gray head and yellow-edged feathers. About forty yards away from the rosewood, the two Shan men were stalking her. While one man was fast approaching from the rear, the other had started to work his way around in front to effectively cut her off.

Brian sprang down the hillside and vaulted over obstacles between the switchbacks so he could descend in a straighter line. Moments later, he hurdled through the last turns of the track and arrived at a long straightaway section which ended near Ellen. Brian had delayed shouting at her, worried that his alarm would provide the Shan with too much time to execute their trap. He could wait no longer. Waiving his machete, he yelled at the top of his lungs. Instantly, the Shan stopped, warning each other at the sight of a wild man closing in on them with fury. From her angle next to the rosewood bush, Ellen could not see Brian, but she heard his shout. There was a snapping noise behind her and she turned around to see one of the Shan only twenty yards away. His malevolent expression terrified her.

Brian came on, gathering speed on the flat ground, gauging the distance to the man in front of Ellen, who was out of her line of sight. The Shan saw that Brian was determined, armed, and strong. He would be able to initiate attacks against them one at a time, improving his odds. Their spears were long and rather than miss a throw, the sturdy pole could be used as a pike to impale an enemy. But the red-bearded man held a machete, a formidable weapon, indeed. If the long knife was swung with enough force and timed correctly, the blade could slice their poles in half. The Shan were experienced warriors; they knew Brian would not hesitate to kill. They called to each other, quickly arriving at the same decision. It was a shame, but the prey was not worth the price they might have to pay. The Shan spun around and broke into a trot at right angles off the path away from Ellen.

Brian raced past Ellen's position, slowing down when he saw the tribesmen running apart. He watched them converging on a low hill far off the trail. They looked back once at him and then disappeared from view. Breathing hard, his adrenaline high, Brian ran back toward Ellen. Already frightened, she caught sight of him bearing down on her and tripped backwards into the tangled rosewood.

"Damn you—why are you here all alone?" he gasped, reaching her at last.

Startled, she shook her head in bewilderment while the comprehension of what had taken place filtered into her mind. His nerves raw, Brian dropped the machete and reaching down, he grabbed her with both hands. The brittle hardwood branches ripped Ellen's blouse as he roughly hauled her out of the bush.

"You bastard, stop manhandling me," she cried.

Panting, hardly able to talk, Brian continued to hold her while he tried to tell her what the natives had planned. The full impact of the Shan's intent hit Ellen, and with a delayed reaction of panic and anger, she tried to wrench free of him. His fever of pent-up anxiety and relief that she was safe goaded Brian all the more.

"What the hell is the matter with you, anyway?" He barked, pulling her tightly against him, believing that no matter what he did she was unreachable.

The fear of what had nearly happened to her caused Ellen to struggle against him. Reflexively, she doubled up her fists and fought him, desperately trying to break his hold on her. In his frustration, Brian buried his face in her hair and she ceased fighting. For a moment they hung together. When she quivered in his arms Brian released her. He saw the anguish in her face, the tears in her eyes and he was disgusted with himself and the impediments between them that he had further complicated.

"Was that necessary...why...?" Ellen said breathlessly. She became aware of her exposure to him and slowly pulled up her damaged blouse, cross-tying the loose ends. As Brian watched helplessly, a resigned sadness spread over Ellen's features.

"We don't even like each other much," she spoke again softy, as if to herself.

Brian was unprepared for this reaction from her. His big hands hung limply at his sides and he felt deflated.

"Ellen, I didn't mean to hurt you...forgive me...but if I'd been a few minutes later..." He was unable to go further.

Ellen stared at him, her eyes luminous and penetrating, with the realization of how much this man cared for her and what he had done on her behalf. The tenuousness of life crossed her mind.

Uncharacteristically, Ellen found herself unable to check her rising emotions.

"I know you don't feel anything for me," he said dully.

"Please don't put words in my mouth," she said.

"Then why can't you give me some indication of...?"

"Brian, we have only known each other a few days!"

"Well, I guess that's been enough for me," he sighed ruefully.

Ellen laughed and there was a transformation between them which allowed each to see the other in a clearer perspective than before. Brian's strained demeanor left him.

"I think we better get out of here," he said. She nodded, and he picked up her backpack.

Brian took her hand and they started up toward the crest of the hill. At the top they saw Min and one of the German boys hurrying toward them. While they waited, Ellen took out her canteen and bending down, tried to clean up the blood and dirt on his knee with a spare handkerchief. The touch of her fingers was soothing, but the gesture meant more. When Min arrived Brian told him about the ambush and fumed at the guide for his carelessness in allowing the Thai assistant to leave the end of the line. The distressed guide immediately offered excuses.

"I must lead all day and arrive at night ready to help cook our meals. I am only one guide with many responsibilities. What do you expect of me?" Min said loudly.

"We expect leadership!" Brian shouted back, advancing toward Min. "That means watching out for everybody. You call yourself a soldier. Do you realize the danger this woman was in, being out all alone?"

"You have no right to say these things to me!" Min protested defiantly.

Ellen stepped between them, her hand on Brian's arm. "Please don't argue any more over something that was really my fault," she pleaded. "It's over and I'm all right. You are a good guide," she reassured Min, who continued to glare at the Americans with resentment.

The four of them moved forward at a rapid pace to join the others who were sitting in a shaded area on the trail.

The worried Italian girls rushed over to Ellen and hugged her. The rest gathered around Brian while the German boy who had accompanied Min gave them details of the Shan ambush before Ellen stopped him with a negative shake of her head. There were grumblings of discontent from the tourists. Min did his best to whitewash the incident while absolving himself of any blame. He assured his party it was an accident they had encountered these particular Shan, who at worst were only mavericks motivated by robbery. Ellen had been in no real physical danger, Min added, since the Shan knew the rest of her group were close by. Ellen kept Brian quiet, convincing him no purpose could be served now by arguing for the truth.

By mid-afternoon the party got underway again, this time bunched closer together with Min's assistant back in the rear. During their final rest stop, Ellen insisted on attending to Brian's damaged knee more thoroughly. She borrowed a tube of antibiotic ointment from the Israeli woman and, taking out a bandage from her own kit, she carefully dressed the wound.

"We are quite different," she declared out of nowhere, in a subdued voice.

"Is that so bad? Maybe that's the spark which has been lacking in our past relationships," he countered.

Ellen stood up and plucked a honeysuckle from its vine. Absently, she looked down at him while tasting the sweetness, her lips drawing out the nectar.

"You know, Brian, men often find me rather cold," she said doggedly, as if testing him.

"Then they must be blind if they can't see the fire under all that defensive armor," he answered, his eyes bright, while he regarded her intently.

This seemed to fluster her and she looked away from his gaze. Then, with a strange uneasy laugh, she said, "You really don't know me at all. How could you?"

"I know enough, Ellen—and the rest doesn't matter right now," he replied with conviction.

Her eyes flickered. She looked down at him again and then turned away, not responding before Min ordered that they get started on their final push to the last village.

In twilight, the line of tourists came down a gradually sloping trail onto a flat plateau. There were the familiar dung smells and whiffs of rising smoke signifying another village not far away. Thankful the hardest hiking was over, the tourists trudged into the camp and were greeted with anticipation by the Red Lahu people who looked forward to the novelty of socialization with foreigners. Since the construction of huts for lodging in this village was on a smaller scale, the party divided up, with Brian and Ellen bunking down with their Israeli friends. After unloading the backpacks, the group was escorted to a wash-up area and then to a community dwelling for the evening meal.

The Red Lahu were a healthy tribe with a love for wearing jingling metal ornaments sewn over much of their brightly colored clothing. After dinner, the group arranged themselves in a circle around the open fire with their hosts. Min spoke with enthusiasm about the village and the ideals of the Red Lahu people, hoping to bury the conduct of the Shan.

"Folks, this tribe only believes in happy spirits. No bad spirits co-exist here as with the other tribes we have seen. In the Red Lahu tribe, everyone mixes," Min declared. "If either a man or woman wants to break their mating bond, they have only to give the equivalent of seven American dollars to the chief; then they are free to find someone else. In this open society, without deceit, no Red Lahu man or woman ever lies about anything, including sex preferences—it is their custom."

"Sure," cried one of the pragmatic German boys, "with divorce so cheap, there is no need to lie!"

There was much laughter around the fire as the relaxed tourists blended in well with the natives while Min translated the questions and answers. The Red Lahu inquired about specific family customs of the four countries represented at their campfire and then everyone sang songs to honor the final night of a difficult journey.

Brian and Ellen talked to the Israeli couple for a few minutes before bedtime, thankful for the extra space and quiet in their hut. It was not so chilly as the previous night and Brian started to lay his bed roll off by himself in one corner of the hut. He was physically and emotionally drained and this brought a calm acceptance to the common ground they had established. Ellen observed his deliberate movements with affection.

"Aren't we going to share security blankets?" she said artfully.

Heartened, Brian glanced up at her and said: "Do you want to?"

"Of course," Ellen said decisively. She dropped to her knees and arranged her bedding next to him. They took off most of their clothes in the darkness and crawled in beside each other. Soon, the exhausted couple across the room fell asleep while Brian and Ellen clung together and listened to the faint rustling of wind.

"Brian, can we be...sure?" she whispered after a while.

"Let's go with our intuition," he said in a low voice.

"We will probably fight a lot," she ventured. "We do seem to have a tendency to misread each other."

"Well, we are getting better at it, aren't we? And think of the excitement which will come from practicing," he said, his voice husky.

Ellen pressed against him and the passion between them welled up as he wrapped his arms round her.

"In fact, we may drive each other crazy," she murmured, stroking his bearded chin with gentle fingers.

"Maybe," he said, his hand caressing her cheek, "but I believe there will be only happy spirits between us."

"Would you ever decide to hand over seven dollars to get rid of me?" Ellen breathed into his ear, her teeth biting his earlobe.

"Never. You'd probably cut my throat first," he said, kissing her hair, her neck, and then her mouth.

Outside, the campfire embers slowly died. Lost in the unity of each other, they did not hear the calling of night birds soaring low over the village toward a rising moon.

A Fair Exchange

LTHOUGH IT HAS BEEN YEARS since our discovery, in my mind I can still picture the street urchin who led me back over thirty thousand years into the past. His name was Roberto and, I suppose, he was about twelve years old the first time I met him. It was hard to tell actually, because when the boy looked directly at me without blinking, as was his custom, he seemed to be a reincarnation of a wise old man. Roberto himself had no idea of his age and origins because he was an orphan, the child of everybody and nobody, in the Andalusian town of Rhonda nestled in the mountains above the southern coast of Spain.

I was a young, unknown archaeologist in those days, specializing in the rather esoteric field of Paleolithic cave art. My career had begun with cataloging prehistoric paintings of Stone Age people who had lived in the ancient rock caves of France and Spain. This job, sparsely funded, required me to take the cave drawing finds of others and arrange them in order of design, pattern, color and age. Frankly, a lot of it was routine work but I enjoyed the time I was given to develop my skills as a speleologist with cave explorations; first in the Dordogne Valley of France, then Altamira in northern Spain, and now here. I realized that my future prospects were rather limited because of a lack of scientific recognition. I had, after all, plowed no new ground nor contributed anything substantial to my field. So I continued to

69

work as a water carrier for better-known men. For a long while I was content to learn my craft and acquire the needed field experience for greater assignments, but by the time I met Roberto one hot afternoon, I was restless and ready for a change in my life.

Andalusia is famous for its wine. I was down in the dumps and had been drinking quite a bit of local stock at the cafe La Pileta, named for a noteworthy Prehistoric cave in the district. This run-down establishment was situated off a side street at the edge of a canyon. While sitting on a wooden bench shaded by a trellis of grape vines, I enjoyed the view of the valley below, dotted with low, square houses of stone on the hot dry land that was overgrazed by sheep and goats.

I had been watching a herd of sheep bleating along the dirt path that zig-zagged up from the valley to a larger roadway near the cafe. It was then that I spied an agile, sure-footed boy scampering over white granite rocks, keeping the animals in line. He was whistling to the sheep while running around their flanks as a sheep dog would do. When they reached the road, an older shepherd came out of the cafe, gave him a coin, and waved him away impatiently. Suddenly, the boy was standing in front of me. I was struck by the quick intelligence reflected in the boy's round, sunburned face. His large, dark eyes never turned away from mine as we regarded each other.

"What your name, señor?" the boy said brashly, in passable English.

"Travers," I answered, looking at his ragged clothes. Then I asked him in Spanish if he lived close by the tavern.

We talked for a while in Spanish and English and after I had passed inspection, the boy introduced himself as Roberto. I

motioned to the cafe owner to bring Roberto a cold soft drink
which he did, scowling at the boy with disapproval. Roberto sat
down next to me. He had big plans, he said. If only he could make
a few initial contacts he would be able to work the tourist trade
at the local hotels. Roberto told me he expected to become very
rich as a guide because he was a hard worker. I liked the boy's
enthusiasm. It was infectious. I laughed at his serious business
manner and his dreams at a time when I felt my own professional
life was stagnant.

In the weeks which followed, Roberto and I became good
friends, which means we trusted each other. I practiced my Spanish while helping him with his English pronunciation, a skill
which he was convinced would open all doors to success. Roberto was a quick study. He learned rapidly because of his tireless
curiosity about everything, including archaeology. Eventually, I
inquired at the local magistrates office to see if the boy could work
with me carrying supplies to the known caves in the district. With
the bored expression of most bureaucrats, the magistrate shrugged
his shoulders in assent. For many months Roberto stayed at my
place while I charted and cataloged rock art. I bought him clothes,
sturdy shoes and gave him a small allowance because he added
to the efficiency of my work. In a sense, I considered Roberto my
partner and, in truth, we grew rather close.

Occasionally, I would take out my old car and go off explor-
ing for a new cave. Sometimes while Roberto was crawling along
a rock escarpment beside me I would catch him looking at me
strangely, in an expectant way. It was as if he wanted to tell me
something useful but was not quite ready to do so.

Once I asked him, "What's on your mind, Roberto?"

"Mmm, nothing, Señor Travers, I just see you only like the picture caves," he said in a deliberate tone.

"Well, of course that's true, Roberto, otherwise one cave is like another. The picture caves represent my work," I added with a confidence I did not feel.

"But some caves with pictures on walls you not like so much as others?" he suggested further.

"It's not that I don't like them all, Roberto, but the ones with fewer pictures—or with the same animal pictures as other caves—give me less of a story of life in the primitive time," I replied, thinking of the caves Roberto had already seen while in my employ. I explained that the essential purpose of my cataloging was to find a common thread of prehistoric life in Europe before the last Ice Age.

Roberto appeared for a while to accept my explanations, yet the pragmatic boy clearly thought my job sketching the oxide and pigment rock drawings to scale on paper was a very tedious and unproductive pastime. There were days when I agreed with him, convinced that I did not have the proper temperament for scientific study. Roberto was especially solicitous when he watched me lying on my back up high in some inaccessible cavern taking photos or hand copying a small drawing.

"Why every picture important?" Roberto asked one day after a particularly hard session in a narrow cave. I had hurt my shoulder on a sharp limestone outcropping and did not respond. This had been an unrewarding day and I was discouraged on the dusty drive back to camp. Roberto never missed my moods and he instinctively knew when to be quiet. When we arrived, I pulled out a catalogue of drawings which showed locations of the great caverns of Spain and France.

"Look, Roberto," I said, pointing to the prehistoric drawings of mammoths, horses, bears and those engravings apparently representing men disguised as animals. "These pictures represent a way of life for people who lived thousands of years ago. Every drawing tells us a story," I added, in an attempt for some self-justification of what we were doing together.

Roberto was interested, but his inquiring mind had moved into other avenues. "Can pictures make you rich—a famous man?"

I grinned at him. "Nobody gets rich in archaeology, but a few important caves have made people famous by their discovery."

I showed the boy a few brightly colored scenes of animals from the magnificent Lascaux cave in France.

Roberto flipped the pages of my catalogue. "These have many more pictures than we have seen," he remarked dryly.

"Yes, each of these well-known caves has its own charm and identity," I said wistfully as we sat together.

The boy turned to a page with a reindeer, an animal we had seen on the wall of one of our caves. I pointed to a fence drawing consisting of a patchwork of straight black lines in the picture.

"Roberto," I continued, "We think the early people used these animals for food and clothing. They were hunters and may even have kept domestic livestock." I waited for this to sink in. "They were cold much of the time and probably afraid, too," I added for effect.

There was no question in my mind that Roberto had great faculties of observation, but his interest had to be piqued with some relevance to the present for him to become fully engaged.

"That has happened to me," the boy said in a low, somber voice, giving me his take on life as an orphan.

"Roberto, by learning from the past we may better understand ourselves," I said grandly. After a moment of silence I took another tack.

"Listen, do you know what 'mana' means?" I paused while fetching two bowls of hot mutton stew I had been brewing on my stove. I laid out some hard bread, purchased that morning for our supper. The boy broke his bread with deliberation and dipped the crust into the thick, brown soup. His eyes flicked up at me.

"Yes, Señor Travers, it means a terrible strong thing." Roberto then commented on what he knew about bullfighting, equating the matador and the bull with his concept of mana.

"It also means the power of the soul, Roberto."

"Ah...in the head?" the boy asked, swallowing a large mouthful of stew. Then he raised his large eyes again.

"Yes, like the spirit Father Crispi talks about in your holy church on Sunday."

Roberto winced. He spent little time in church, a fact of which the local priest was quite aware.

I returned to my catalog and, holding it up from the table, I pointed to those drawings featuring wild animals with human arms and legs. Roberto looked at the heads of a group of reindeer, mouths open, racks of horns tilted forward ready to defend themselves.

"We think the ancient people who drew these pictures believed that the spirit of a great animal—mana—could be captured and this magic would assist them in their hunt for food."

I could see that this sober boy from the streets found my high-minded lecture hard to accept, but the fact that I believed what

I was saying was enough for him. After supper we sat outside for a while and looked at the moonlight illuminating a grove of olive trees. There was the faint sound of guitar music from the cafe. I lit a cigar, and in the quiet of the night there was an awareness of each other as kindred spirits. To me, the force, the mana, of our respective wills blended in the brightness of a full moon. After a while we talked of the caves again.

"Roberto," I said finally, "we think the caves were considered to be places of sanctuary—holy places for the ancients. Perhaps the artists, priests, or medicine men who drew the pictures would not even allow the ordinary members of tribes to see them. There are many theories about all this, but I think the caves with paintings were sacred."

One day, near the end of our time together, Roberto and I were working in a cave with crude representations of men hunting. They were depicted as charcoal stick drawings. Even these primitive, straight-line figures of people were not common in most of the known caves and none ever had the beautiful composition and proper proportion of the animal drawings. I explained all this to Roberto.

He became very curious. "Why were the human figures never as good as the animals, and why didn't they have faces?" he wondered. It was a logical question.

"This is a mystery to us," I told him. "It is thought that perhaps these early artists were afraid to have a complete drawing made of human faces and bodies because this could mean that that person's soul was lost—that his spirit would be trapped in the cave forever by the painting."

Roberto returned to our discussion of mana and he asked, "Then why were there half-animal and half-men pictures?"

I knew this appeared to be a contradiction to him. I said, "Well, maybe it was all right if a man was shown only from the waist down with an animal for a head." I reminded Roberto how some people in his own country did not allow tourists to take their photos.

Neither of us spoke for a moment. Then I added, "Remember, I told you that all this art was probably a religion to these ancient people. It is possible a priest or shaman controlled what was drawn in the caves."

Roberto was thoughtful. "So, someone like Father Crispi wanted no faces," he remarked seriously.

"That is what some of us think," I said, smiling at the boy and roughing up his black hair with my hand.

Roberto had been a fine companion. There was both fondness and empathy between us, and I knew we would miss each other after my departure from Spain. We had talked about my going home. I had told him his English was now good enough to work the tourist trade. In fact, I had already spoken highly of Roberto's character with those local business owners who dealt with tourists, particularly at the hotels.

The days passed and on a late spring evening I began the long process of gathering all my notes and charts together for packing. Roberto came to my room. His expression was one of both sadness and expectation while he stood at attention in front of me.

The boy took a deep breath and I saw a profound look in his eyes. "Señor Travers, we have found no famous caves with the beautiful colored pictures, have we?"

"No, Roberto, but we have done some good work together and I am grateful to have had you by my side," I said.

Roberto did not move. There was silence in the room except for the rustling of papers as I continued to pack. Then he said quietly, "Señor Travers, I am ready now to show you my secret."

"What secret?" I asked, my hands still busy.

"One I tell no one, until now," the boy responded.

"All right, Roberto, what is it." I said, pushing away a box that I had just filled.

"My secret is a special cave. It has many pictures you have not seen," he blurted out in a rush.

Roberto had my attention.

"Wait a minute. You want me to look at a cave on the maps that we have not looked at before?"

"No," he said firmly, "my cave is not on the maps."

I felt light-headed from a gnawing sense of excitement and for a moment I was speechless.

"Roberto, you mean you found a cave with paintings that is not known?"

"Yes, Señor Travers, a cave no one in this world but me has ever seen. I find it when I take care of the sheep—now, you must stay."

I could not believe what I was hearing. Recovering at last, I fired a number of questions at the boy. All Roberto would say was that two years ago, while tending sheep in a canyon, he had discovered a small hidden entrance to a deep cave with prehistoric art. He told me that he had crawled a short distance into the cave only twice, the second time with a candle. Apparently, he had become afraid of the inky darkness. What I found uncharacteristic of Roberto, was that he seemed uneasy over what he had seen on the walls of the cave.

"Señor Travers," he said in low voice, "you are my friend, I show you where cave is, but much magic there—many spirits."

Roberto was usually unconcerned about cave superstitions, so his demeanor was surprising and provoked my rising anticipation. I was afraid that the possibility of a dramatic archaeological find would overpower my usual calm approach toward cave exploration.

At dawn the next morning we packed food and water and drove to the far north of town. Leaving the paved road, we continued for about an hour along a rough dirt track. Roberto finally indicated where he wanted me to stop. I unloaded my spelunking gear, divided up the ropes between us and stuffed two head lamps into my backpack. We began a difficult hike with Roberto leading the way over a series of harsh granite escarpments. Occasionally, the boy would pause, get his bearings, and then scamper off in a new direction. At midday we sat down for lunch. I was somewhat disheartened and considered the fact that Roberto might not really know what he was doing.

"Cave not far off now, Señor Travers," he said, looking at me intently. We set off again and soon came down from a ridge of crumbling rock into a narrow canyon. Roberto pointed to a massive outcropping of granite about halfway up the canyon wall on the opposite side. Laboriously we climbed up to this section of rock, but still I could see nothing unusual.

Roberto moved laterally along a tiny sheep trail against the lower face of the cliff until he came to a massive overhanging boulder in front of us. Bending low, he pulled aside a dried-up shrub under the boulder, revealing a hole.

"I hide cave with bush after one of my lambs fall in," he cried, breathlessly.

I edged toward him and saw a rather small triangular opening between two flat rock slabs. It appeared to me that the huge boulder had once been much higher on the cliff and had fallen down. This displacement wedged the rock slabs almost together, reducing the original size of the opening.

Roberto dramatically stood at the entrance. Pointing at the hole, he said, "Now, Señor Travers, you will see people who look like people."

I could not imagine what Roberto was trying to tell me as we took out our head lamps. Plunking his own hat firmly on his head and flicking on the light, he crawled into the opening. I followed with some uncertainty and was soon on my chest, squirming along behind the boy. This was clearly an unexplored cave with uneven projections, loose dirt and cobwebs everywhere. After about fifteen yards, the narrow tunnel widened into a small limestone cavern where we could barely stand. Roberto removed our one large flashlight and played his light over the walls.

Before I had a chance to look, there was a thick mass of black hurling at my face. We fell to the ground amid a series of high-pitched screeches. Frightened bats, wings beating frantically, rapidly flew off away from us and disappeared farther inside the tunnel.

"There is probably another exit at the far side of the hill," I cried, feeling a slight tinge of circulating air from both ends of the shaft.

The dust the bats kicked up had settled, and my eyes focused again on Roberto. The boy shined his light on the walls flanking the opening in front of us. Gently, he touched my arm. "Look, señor," he said in a hushed tone, "is it not what I tell you?"

I held my breath, not believing what I saw reflected by our lights. On each side of the entryway in front of us were paintings of two life-sized prehistoric hunters holding barbed spears aimed at the ceiling. They were anything but the usual crudely-formed figures of people who occupied caves in the Stone Age. These two-dimensional human bodies were exquisitely drawn. I moved closer and looked up.

Over the entrance, above the heads of the hunters, a smooth rock lintel displayed a pictograph of stars. I was astonished. I was sure this celestial diagram represented a solstice celebration of some kind. Never before had I seen such evidence of spiritual symbolism in the Stone Age.

"My God, Roberto! What have you found?" I exclaimed, peering closely at the entryway.

The boy bent low under the arch that separated the two hunters. "Señor Travers, look at this." His voice echoed from the other side of the next room.

Pulling myself away reluctantly, I joined him deeper in the cave. His lights were now on the ceiling revealing a parade of animals painted in black, red, and yellow pigments. Along an open rock face galloped herds of horses, bison, and reindeer pursued by hunters. The boy turned and directed the light on the walls in back of me. I saw a group of hairy mammoths, their enormous curved tusks held high, charging the opening we had just passed through in the soundless cavern.

The art work ranked above the finest I had viewed anywhere. I judged the paintings to be of the Solutrean period, about 35,000 years in age.

I turned to the boy. "Roberto, you have discovered something of great importance. I...can't believe my eyes."

Roberto smiled, "It is good; no, señor?"

"The best I have ever seen," I said, shining my head lamp over the figures.

"I think there is more, Señor Travers," Roberto said. He moved away from me to the far end of this section of the cave. The impatience of the young, I thought, not wanting to tear myself away. After all, Roberto had seen this part of the cave before. Yet, as I came alongside the boy, I sensed that he did not seem quite so confident.

"Señor, I never been farther than this—I was afraid."

"I can see why, Roberto," I remarked. The floor was now damp. Beyond, it sloped downward at an alarming angle.

I considered the fact we were out here alone with no one aware of our location. It was not safe. I suggested that we should turn back and get others to help us.

Neither of us actually wanted to leave. "Señor Travers," the boy cried, "I not want anyone to see all of my cave before us."

Too easily, I was persuaded to continue. "Okay, Roberto," I said abruptly. "Let's see if we can go a little farther."

I decided to anchor our rope to a solid stalagmite stump projecting upward from the floor where we stood. The cavern was cool with air coming up from below, but I was perspiring heavily. I went off first down the rope after tucking the flashlight into my belt. The boy followed a few yards behind. Reaching the bottom, I saw that the shaft abruptly turned and was narrowed by a scree of rock partially blocking the passage. The rock had probably fallen long after the Pleistocene inhabitants had left because I could make out the remains of a broken stairway.

Wet slime from an underground water source hindered my progress while I tried to find decent foot holds.

"Roberto," I called back, "be careful, around this rock slide. It's very slippery."

Wiggling around the new angle of the tunnel, I saw that it would be necessary to climb downward again within a chimney of more solid rock. We jammed our backs into the sides of the chimney while I anchored a new line of rope. I was happy to find that the rock was becoming dry again, making it easier to move. Suddenly, my knapsack caught on a jagged piece of rock, throwing me off balance, and I fell. Grabbing the rope, I corkscrewed down the funnel out of control until I crashed on top of a pile of loose gravel littered on the ground below.

For a moment I blacked out. Then I heard Roberto yelling from above me.

"Señor, señor! Are you hurt? Where are you?" There was fear in his voice.

"Over here, Roberto. I'm okay, I think. Be careful coming down the rope."

Quickly, the agile boy dropped down near me and I could see the last of our rope dangling just above us where I had let it go. I sat up and realized my head lamp was broken. Reaching into the pack I pulled out one of our magnesium flares and lit it on the floor. The cavern was bathed in bright reflected light and we could see that this new gallery was huge.

It was as if we had entered a cathedral with vaulted ceilings and rock pillars all around us. Outcroppings of limestone appeared as draperies along some of the walls. While I held the flare up high, the boy and I started to walk along a clean, dry pathway into the heart of the room.

Nothing in my professional career had prepared me for the panoramic scenes all around us. Enormous wall paintings of people revealed life in prehistoric times that I had never imagined existed. The art was extraordinary in detail, creating a visual depth that made the pictures come alive. The scenes were clear, passionate but also mystical with a powerful blending of imagery and ideas of the past.

Roberto and I did not speak as we saw a procession of well-muscled men holding hands, their primitive, bearded faces were turned toward a common center on the great wall in front of us. The scene was one of a tribal ceremony of devotion or homage. In the center of the drawing on a raised dais stood a full-sized figure of a nude woman holding up a child with both hands in supplication. The beautiful, natural composition of the men and woman was staggering to me. The woman's face displayed a graceful dignity that belied my preconceived notions of Stone Age people. Was she a queen or high priestess? Was I looking at a prehistoric fertility rite within this rock sanctuary?

Roberto and I held hands while we moved along the walls trying to capture the entire theme of the painting. We saw a procession of males standing opposite a line of females who were extending their arms toward them. The dimensions and artistic perspective of their faces could have come from our own time. Clearly, these people were more than unsophisticated Ice Age survivalists. This was Paleolithic art without precedence.

Roberto spoke at last. "People here are real—no, señor? Not like we see in other caves."

"Nothing like this exists anywhere that we know of, Roberto. This discovery will change our understanding of the ancients," I said quietly.

"So, men of books wrong sometimes," Roberto offered without sarcasm or self-importance.

"More than sometimes, Roberto." I put my arm around the boy and squeezed hard. He saw that there were tears in my eyes, and he laughed at me in a boyish way as if anything in the world was possible.

"Now you be famous," he said. There was a broad grin on his face.

The magnesium torch hissed and I lit my last one, passing it to Roberto. Rapidly, I began to take photos feeling as though I was desanctifying a sacred shrine of these prehistoric people. Soon, I thought it best to leave while we still had good light. Returning to the rope, we put our equipment in order and struggled up, back toward the opening of the cave. I took a few more pictures of the cave and then we went out into the sunlight to a world which would not be the same again for either of us.

The news of what was to be called "Travers' Cave" spread quickly, and the site now has a paved road leading to a guarded entrance designed for archaeologists, government officials, and selected tourists. My reputation was assured and, as Roberto had predicted, I am considered to be an authority in my field.

As for Roberto, I haven't seen him in years. I sponsored his education at the University of Madrid, where he did not study archaeology of course, but rather economics and government. I understand his having little time for the kinds of things we used to do together. It is difficult for a high government minister and wealthy landowner to have much time for a stodgy professor, no matter how famous.

Awakening

I T WAS LATE IN THE AFTERNOON and Andrews had been climbing steadily over the past four hours. His physical condition was growing worse, and each breath delivered a searing pain to his oxygen-starved lungs. The effort of sucking in the icy, thin air caused a persistent wheezing noise and he listened to the sound with detachment, as if it were coming from someone else. Andrews fought to keep up with Jung, his tenacious Sherpa guide working high above him, chiseling out narrow steps on the glass wall of snow and ice.

Jung was small, but he climbed tirelessly while chopping out the flakes, swinging his ice ax with fluid precision. Occasionally, he would use his ax to set a piton for the rope which dangled down to the American and the heavily loaded porters below. Andrews found it was better to keep his eyes on Jung rather than looking down. Below the party, a glacial moraine fell away toward the rock-strewn Modi Khola gorge, carved by Nepal's mighty Kali Gandaki River. A biting wind rose from this canyon, deepest in the world, the sides only twenty miles apart, creating an enormous funnel which allowed the wind to gather power and then project upward between the Dhulagiri and Annapurna massifs.

These giants, Dhulagiri to the west of the river and Annapurna to the east, each over 26,000 feet high, flanked the gorge.

Andrews listened to the mournful howling of the wind as he labored with despair in his heart, knowing he was not going to get much closer to Annapurna than the ridge they were now approaching. A swath of brilliant whiteness spread out in the shape of an immense fan around the climbers strung out on the glacier. Eventually, the team of men traversed a dangerous pitch encrusted with ice in order to reach a granite chute. Jung snapped out a longer section of nylon line and, looping it over a rock projection, he called for a belay for greater stability. Andrews was unsteady from an attack of vertigo while he set the rope. He waited, panting in short, quick, labored breaths and then resumed the climb behind his guide. Crossing a snow bridge that Jung had tested for compaction, Andrews was sick again from the waves of nausea that gripped him.

"Mr. Andrews...you okay?" Jung called down, his Mongolian features accentuated by goggles reflecting the fading sunlight. "Shall we stop for a while?" He asked again.

"No...no, let's go on; we're losing our light," Andrews replied in a ghostly voice.

He was desperate to sit down and rest, to suspend the agony, because he was close to passing out. Yet, Andrews realized that if he ordered a halt too soon he would not be able to start again. Besides, the party was in an unsuitable place to stop for the night. While Jung resumed the job of cutting out steps, Andrews methodically concentrated on setting one boot in front of the other. He jabbed the pointed end of his ice ax alongside each step, using the ax more as a cane than as a lever for proper support. The chunk, chunk sounds drummed in his ears while the team made their way ever higher along the roof of the world.

Andrews had begun his pilgrimage to the Annapurna Mountain Sanctuary with his wife, Emily, who had planned to accompany her husband while they were in the lowlands. The sanctuary was an enchanting realm of mystical beauty for the couple. At the lower altitudes, veiled misty clouds from the uplands had shrouded the track into menacing snow fields which lay far above the valleys. Andrews was fifty and, although he had prepared for his odyssey by training in the mountains of North America, he was no match for the arduous demands of a serious Himalayan climb. He never really expected to climb one of the major peaks—for that he would have needed a full-scale expedition along with the talent and stamina of a younger man—but he had wanted to come within a respectable distance to the base of Annapurna.

At the moment he was far away from his mountain, although he could see its upper flanks and pyramid top in bold relief. Andrews estimated the ridge they were drawing near to was about 16,000 feet, perhaps a little less. It had been the frequent elevation changes that had proven to be too much for him. Climbing in Nepal was punishing. He had hiked up steep elevations and then rapidly descended into deep valleys, only to ascend another mountain near the same elevation in order to progress higher toward his goal. The resignation of defeat which had crept over Andrews after all this effort was coupled with a sense of futility about his dream of ever reaching Annapurna.

Weary beyond what he could have imagined, his mind drifted in and out of the present to when he last saw his wife. Did Emily feel his thoughts now? Perhaps at this very moment she was looking in his direction. Before she had returned to their original staging area in the Pokhara Valley with two of the porters, Emily had pressed her hands against his cheeks and told him that she knew he would be able to do whatever was necessary to realize his dream, but that it was more important he come back to her safely. She kissed him goodbye tenderly. Emily's brave expression could not mask her anxiety because she was unable to hide her tears. Quickly, she had turned away and left him then, waving one last time on the track down the mountain before disappearing from his sight.

Andrews thought about their days together before the climb, when they had poked around the medieval bazaar towns of Kathmandu and Patan. His mind still held the images of golden pagoda temples and fret-worked wooden houses leaning toward each other across narrow cobblestone streets. He imagined himself again holding Emily's hand as they excitedly pushed their way through the wandering sacred cows, holy men, flute players, beggars and all the merchants hawking rugs, brass pots and vibrant garments. Everything was a kaleidoscope of color and activity stretching back to an earlier age, transforming Andrews into an embodiment of someone other than himself.

By the time preparations for the climb had been completed, his mind was possessed by Annapurna. Emily had been at his side on the track through the lowland villages, past the fishtailed pinnacle of sacred Machhapuchare which heralded his way forward. They had laughed together on the stone stairway between Naudandanda and Chandrakot watching Tibetan tribesmen driving their brightly tasseled mule caravans loaded with hides and wool to exchange for such staples as rice and tea in the lowland market towns. Long metal bells with bone clappers were attached to the neck yokes of these animals and they gave off a resonant gong sound, announcing their coming to others moving around switchbacks on the trail. It was a scene unchanged for centuries on the established trade route from Tibet where the Mongol-Buddhist people of the mountains mixed with Aryan-Hindus living in the terraced lowlands.

As the foothills grew steeper, Andrews and his wife passed stair-stepped Buddhist shrines adorned with flapping banners. They heard the chanting of prayers accompanied by noisy prayer wheels. These etched metallic cylinders, which squeaked merrily, could be spun for luck by travelers and Emily had taken his hand in hers to perform this ritual. In the early stages of the journey, they had spent nights bunked in foul smelling animal courtyards, or under low-ceiling rooms choked with smoke from the cooking fires. Emily had been completely engrossed with the events of each day, while Andrews was preoccupied by the mountains ahead. He remembered Emily's fascination for the Newari women weaving sheep's wool on primitive looms and hugging him with delight after he bought her a brightly colored scarf for a few rupees.

In the beginning, as his adventure was at last unfolding, Andrews felt a surge of rejuvenation as if he were young again. He had chosen the legendary Annapurna for his quest because stories about the mountain had captivated him during his boyhood days when the world learned of the first ascent by two gallant Frenchmen in 1950. These mountaineers had returned frostbitten, losing parts of their hands and feet as the price for victory on the highest mountain then climbed by anyone. Andrews and his best friend imagined themselves going to Annapurna as a team on an adventure which would carry them away from their ordinary lives into this exotic place. Hiking in the hills around their homes they convinced each other that if they could get to

the highest mountains of the world, this feat would be ennobling
and liberating at the same time. As young men of limited resources
and eventually family responsibilities they never went to Nepal
together. When his best friend died in middle age of alcoholism,
Andrews told his wife that he could not let their dream also die
as a goal never realized. If he could even get close to Annapurna, it would be the capstone of his life for all his unrealized ambi-
tions and a tribute to the memory of his friend.

Jung pulled the rope taut and the hard jerk forced Andrews
to come awake.

"We will make camp here!" the Sherpa guide shouted down
from the top of the ridge.

"That's fine, Jung," Andrews sighed gratefully. Slowly, with
grim determination he reached the lip of the ridge and rolled over
in the snow.

He was on a small plateau, shaped like a bowl, nestled below
a tumbled mass of broken ice blocks that would provide shelter
from the wind. While Annapurna could be seen far off to the right,
the track ahead of them contained a steep pitch with an overhanging cornice of snow and rock just beyond the seracs around
them. Andrews knew, that for him, the route was impassable. He
would go no higher.

Hardly able to breathe, he shuffled over to Jung and unhooked
himself from the rope while the guide returned to help the porters.
Dropping to his knees from altitude sickness, his ears ringing,
Andrews removed his backpack and then sat down in the snow,
taking off the crampons on his boots. While resting, he raised his
binoculars and watched the white plumes of an avalanche cas-
cading down the upper flanks of Annapurna in the fading twilight.

The mountain was dangerous and yet he still felt a sense of desolation because it seemed as if its peak was beckoning him.

The sweating porters soon arrived one by one over the ridge onto the plateau. Removing their bulging packs containing all the provisions, they unloaded everything with rapid efficiency. The tents were set up and preparations for the evening meal began. While Andrews observed the porters, he considered the fact that each man had carried at least three times the weight on their backs than he had that day. The men chatted happily at their work and the thought occurred to the American that they were children of the mountains. He saw himself as an outsider who did not belong among them in this dazzling, perilous domain.

When his own tent was ready, Andrews crawled in and collapsed on his sleeping bag, unable to move. In a stupor, he felt his spirit floating away, steered by the wind toward the great tower. Nightfall closed in on the camp and Jung came through the flaps of his tent as an apparition. He handed his client a tin cup of hot, scented tea.

"You are not feeling so well, Mr. Andrews?" The guide was solicitous, but quite matter-of-fact. It was not really a question at all, but the statement of a problem which required solving. Jung squatted down on his heels, Nepalese fashion, and lit his pipe. He was a Tamang of Tibetan origin with high cheekbones and steady opaque eyes that revealed nothing while assessing his client's torment.

"No, Jung," he answered with lassitude, "the truth is, I'm not doing too well…sorry. I don't think I am capable of going on tomorrow." He sounded pathetic to himself, the frustration worse inside him now that his failure was admitted openly.

Jung did not acknowledge Andrews' words for a few moments as he smoked quietly and looked away into the depths of closing darkness. The American tried again.

"You know, Jung, I very much wanted greater success from this climb...I mean to get further up...to prove I could do it and meet the challenge..." His voice died in his throat.

The guide leaned forward with an expression of serenity.

"Mr. Andrews, these mountains and the valleys and rivers of this land have been the home of my people for thousands of years. We do not look upon our home as some sort of personal challenge because we were born here and live our whole lives at high altitudes. People come from other lands—not to live here—but to test themselves against the mountains, to prove something perhaps. I do not say this is wrongful—this single-minded purpose to reach high places—but there is so much more to gain."

Jung paused, his hands carefully stroked his pipe before he continued.

"Mr. Andrews, the power of nature is all over the world everywhere, including our own home. Do you not feel it now?"

"Yes, of course I do, Jung," he answered too quickly, unaware that his guide was a disciplined ascetic.

"And, is this feeling not good? Are you not in a distinctive space right here?" the guide persisted.

"Well...yes...and it's been an exhilarating and unique experience too," Andrews replied, his tone strained. "But, I also feel disappointed at not reaching my goal."

"And what is your goal?" Jung asked.

"Well...to go further...nearer to Annapurna, where the real climbers have gone," Andrews said hoarsely, feeling embarrassed and even a little shamed.

"Mr. Andrews, may I speak to you in a direct manner?"

"Certainly, go ahead."

"You are not young and I think you have done well. Do you believe you will be less of a human being because you are unable climb higher?" the guide admonished him gently.

Andrews grew resentful. Pulling himself up on his elbows he exclaimed desperately, "I'm not a quitter. It's the giving up I don't like."

"Tell me," Jung said quietly, "what will our stopping here take away from you that you do not now already have?"

"You ought to know, Jung. The loss of success in achieving a difficult goal. My dream was to reach Annapurna. It is something I have thought about for thirty-five years."

"And what did you expect to find there?"

"I...I can't explain it...to find a source which would define who I am...that the power of the mountain would bring me into a higher state of being," Andrews replied, his anger gradually dissipating.

"I see," Jung said in a soft tone. "You have allowed your desire for Annapurna—an external thing—to determine how you feel about yourself so you will not have to look within to find peace."

"Now, just a minute..."

There was a signal from one of the porters. Jung left Andrews to return shortly with two wooden bowls of steaming noodles, beans and vegetables. Handing a bowl to his client, he started on his own meal. Although the nausea had subsided, Andrews was not particularly hungry. With his guide's encouragement, however, he ate a little and felt stronger.

"Mr. Andrews, you know we are a nation of Buddhists. In my younger days I was educated to be a monk. I left the monastery when I knew I was unworthy and returned to a life of imperfections. We believe emotional attachments to self stand in the way of insight into the true reality of our existence.

"Look, Jung," Andrews said between spoonfuls of his meal, "at home I am not considered to be a self-centered person."

"That is not what I meant, Mr. Andrews. To the Buddhist, the craving, or excessive desire for something, takes away from one's individual freedom by limiting choices for that person. We consider this to be an enslavement of the mind. Permit me to say, I think you have allowed this to happen to you."

"Jung, I resent this! Are you telling me that coming to Nepal in order to reach Annapurna was a mistake because my body is unable to do what my mind desires?"

"No, what I am saying is that the suffering you have already endured is enough to bring you awareness," the guide said evenly. "It is not necessary to go higher. If you cannot find meaning on this plateau and be in harmony with our surroundings here, it is my opinion you would not be able to do so even if you were on top of Annapurna."

Andrews thought about this while he ate a few more spoonfuls of food. His guide lit another pipe and seemed to be in a state of contemplation.

"All right," Andrews said at last, "I understand what you are getting at, but I do believe in goals. You chose not to become a Buddhist monk. You decided instead to guide people up high mountains as a means of earning a living. You must derive satisfaction from this, Jung. So tell me, what does success in life mean to you?"

"I will try. We become whole by a oneness of our spirit with nature, which is everywhere. Man should not do battle with the forces of nature except when his life is at stake. Even then, it is better when we permit these forces to flow peacefully through the senses to achieve balance and harmony with one's surroundings regardless of physical conditions. True success is acting on these principles which brings awareness and happiness to the mind wherever you are."

"And just how do we find that?" Andrews exclaimed bitterly, his despondency and feelings of failure lingering within him still.

"Mr. Andrews, a hungry man sees a fruit tree and climbs up the trunk to the top because he thinks the fruit on the lower branches is too easy and therefore not worthwhile. After he struggles to the top of the tree, he finds the fruit to be just the same. He did not regard the whole tree before he began his ascent. Often what we seek is not ahead of us but actually what we have left behind."

Andrews reflected on the parable and saw that Jung was preparing to leave. With difficulty, he rose from his sleeping bag and left the tent to follow the guide who was walking to the edge of the ridge. The wind had died, and in the stillness Jung swung his arm in a wide circle around their camp and the vast space beyond.

"Enlightenment comes with using all the senses that take us beyond reason. The world may not be as we conceive it in the mind but rather how we feel it. Can you not see we are at one with everything here before us, Mr. Andrews?"

Andrews listened to the silence on the plateau and allowed himself to drink fully of the splendor of the night. Above the massive reach of the Himalayas, his vision absorbed gleaming starlight from the constellations, all unchanged from the time he had seen them above his backyard as a boy.

The melancholy which Andrews had allowed to pervade his being on the raw plateau of snow and ice was gradually replaced by comprehension. Taking a deep breath of the rarefied air, Andrews began to sense his connection with life. Although physically spent, he felt truly whole in this moment, as if the power of the mountains had integrated with his spirit and brought forth a knowing that had always been there.

"It is beautiful, isn't it Jung?" Andrews said finally, the burden of the pact with his best friend released from his mind.

"Yes, everywhere, not just one mountain," the guide said, turning to smile at him, "and you are part of it all."

Andrews laughed, hearing the sound echoing off the crystal walls of the glacial bowl around them. Jung stretched and carefully knocked the ashes out of his pipe against his boot.

"Rest now, Mr. Andrews, and in the days ahead after we get down from this difficult section of the mountain, I will take you on a route back through a fine region of deodars and rhododendrons to rejoin your wife."

Placing the palms of his brown, weathered hands together and bowing slightly toward Andrews in the traditional Nepalese salute, Jung respectfully said, "Namaste!" and walked away to his tent.

Andrews was alone then, but at peace with himself at last. His thoughts turned to Emily, her loving acceptance of his restlessness and the happiness she had given him during their life together. Suddenly, he was anxious to begin his descent in the morning.

The Chief

THE FIRST TIME I SAW the stocky native chief crab-stepping along the pier, swaying from one side to the other, favoring his game leg, my impression was that the man looked nothing at all like a ruler of people. The inter-island supply boat from Suva had just dropped anchor at a broken-down pier on the small island of Lakemba in the outer Lau group of the Fijian Islands. While the crew began off-loading provisions, I collected my skin-diving bag and modest suitcase and, hoisting them onto the uneven wooden planks of the pier, I jumped off the boat. The island port was very quiet, almost deserted except for the chief and a few natives working on the pier. The island seemed to me to be located at the edge of the world, which was exactly what I was seeking.

The chief stopped his inspection tour of the unloading long enough to give me a brief glance.

"Mark," the boat skipper said, appearing at my elbow, "meet the chief of Lakemba. He has a longer, more impressive name as the cousin of the prime minister of all Fiji, but here he answers to the name of Rocco."

"Bula!" the chief said to me in the traditional Fijian greeting.

Rocco cocked his large, bushy head toward me, and I noticed one eye was almost closed in a perpetual squint. The other one measured me with a look of curiosity and perhaps disdain, I wasn't sure.

"Glad to meet you too, chief," I said, noticing his faded khaki shirt and matching baggy tropical shorts. His outfit was reminiscent of an old British colonial official. A well-fed brown belly protruded from the chief's ill-fitting clothes. His sneakers were torn and dirty.

"You underwater fisherman?" Rocco inquired casually, scratching his head while appraising my diving equipment.

"Well—yes, chief, as a matter of fact I am, although I'm a little out of shape," I told him.

"You want to catch big fish?" he said with an air of detachment, squinting over my shoulder at the ocean.

"That would be fine—yes," I nodded, "that's why I'm here."

"You need boat?" Rocco asked, and his expression grew more intense.

"Yes, I suppose so," I said, wondering what other options were available for boat rentals.

"I have boat!" The chief spoke with authority, his fully opened eye scrutinizing me more carefully.

"Take him up on it, Mark," called the skipper, who was moving away toward the cargo. "Rocco loves to fish and he has the only working long boat on the island for sport fishing. I'll be back to pick you up in a few days."

"Tomorrow morning we go catch big fish—you be here early," directed the chief. I felt this was more of a command than an invitation.

Without waiting for my reply, Rocco turned his back on me and continued his personal inspection of the supplies coming off the boat. I shrugged and, picking up my bags, I walked off the pier along a dusty dirt track designated as the main road around the flat island.

The boat captain had told me the only guest house was about a half mile away. The faded white clapboard dwelling had three rooms for rent, all empty. My room was bare except for a single hard cot placed under a hanging turtle shell, but at least there was a paddle fan on the ceiling for circulation. The rooming house was run by a local fisherman's wife who said she was preparing flounder for supper. As evening approached and I finished my meal, the woman advised me that I was to be ready at first light.

"My husband and another man will be going out with you and Rocco, she announced proudly. "Our chief does not like to be kept waiting."

"Do we have to go so early?" I asked her, wondering why such a big production was being made of a simple dive to some near-by reef off the beach. I was supposed to be on vacation, free from time schedules and deadlines.

The Fijian woman frowned at me in disapproval. "Chief Rocco—he like to fish early every day—he great fisherman," she replied in a somber tone, smoothing out the folds of her lava-lava in a manner which indicated the subject was closed.

"Okay, I get the message," I reassured her.

I decided to take a walk along the chalk-white, unspoiled beach strewn with fragments of nautilus and turban shells. I watched a young native in great condition swim ashore and considered how I had let myself go to pot in the two years since my wife had been killed in a car accident. For a long time after Sara's crash, my grief was so overpowering that I only went through the motions of living. My existence just didn't seem to have any meaning anymore, and the only way I could keep my sanity was to plunge into non-stop work. Somehow, I endured without Sara's presence but my zest for life was gone because part of me was missing. My friends in Los Angeles finally convinced me to take a month off and renew my passion for ocean diving. They suggested the South Pacific as the place to come for my first vacation since the accident.

The landlady woke me at dawn.

"Time to go—Rocco ready," she said, setting a bag containing bread and hard-boiled eggs down on my bed.

Hardly awake, I fumbled with my things and decided to leave behind my flotation tube and fish net since I expected to be diving off the boat. My landlady handed me a mango for breakfast and pushed me out the door into the gathering sunrise.

Under a coconut grove near the pier, final preparations were in progress. A freshly-painted, bright red and white wooden long boat with an outboard motor was being readied with bait and fishing tackle. I noticed that the prow of the boat had a crude black drawing of a fierce Fiji war god. The Fijians are a good-humored people who become short tempered and even threatening to outsiders who patronize them. They are a physically strong and brave race. I was not surprised to see the countenance of the war god staring at me.

"You ready?" Rocco appeared suddenly from around the side of the boat. He squinted at my spear gun with anticipation.

"Yeah, I guess so," I said, "but I thought I might sit on the beach and have some breakfast first."

"No time now—fish waiting," the chief said, his thick lips twisted wryly.

The two boatmen shoved the craft down the sand into the water and kicked over the engine. I got in with Rocco and sat down next to one of the large oar locks. The boat rode diagonally across troughs in the surf, snaking out into the still dark sea. I watched the beach receding from view. I was disappointed that there was no placid lagoon protected by a coral reef around the island of Lakemba. Yesterday had been rather calm but as we drove further into the open sea, I realized today was going to be different. Feeling the deep ground swells underneath me, each lifting the boat to new heights, I took hold of the gunwale as we pitched over the waves into ever widening blue trenches.

The chief was standing perfectly balanced on the centerboard while happily trolling, using a variety of lures and live bait. I saw his long fishing line following in the wake of the boat while we twisted and turned amid the spraying foam. His legs planted far apart, Rocco was not bothered by his lameness as he barked orders to the two boatman who continually altered course to appease him.

I remembered the antique Fijian war canoe I had seen at the marine museum in Suva on the main island. They had been called Drubas and were built like enormous catamarans from hollowed-out tree trunks. A big Druba could hold more than a hundred warriors and was owned and commanded only by chiefs on raiding parties or inter-island migrations. As I watched Rocco standing straight up in the lurching boat, waving his arms one way and then another, I thought the chief was acting as though he was commanding a Druba.

The rolling boat had been in deeper water for well over an hour and Lakemba had vanished below the horizon. As the motor chugged away, I grew queasy from the fuel vapors and an empty stomach. Forcing one of the eggs into my mouth, I washed it down with canteen water and came close to vomiting.

The day was turning windy and there was a low bank of gray clouds swirling overhead. The air had the warmth of the tropics, but I shivered from the cresting waves hitting the boat and sloshing over me. Rocco worked diligently with his trolling line but there were no bites.

After a while something dark on the ocean in front of us caught my attention. Soon, a jagged spire appeared to rise up out of the sea. As we drew closer, I saw the rock was shaped like a ship's stern that was sinking almost vertically into the ocean. Our boat coasted near the rock, which was now a shiny black mass in the flat light.

"Ho!" cried Rocco. "We stop."

The motor was shifted into the idle position with a loud clunk.

"Big fish here," Rocco announced. He looked at me in expectation.

I was startled. We were in the middle of nowhere, at least ten miles away from the island. That alone was not a deterrent with the boat nearby, I argued to myself, but it was the lone rock itself sticking out of the water which looked so inhospitable. Rocco sensed my lack of enthusiasm.

"You go!" the chief insisted.

Reluctantly, I stood up while the boat rocked back and forth in the swells. One of the boatmen used an oar to keep us from banging against the rock. I put on my mask, snorkel and fins, feeling a little sick. While I strapped the calf knife in place, my leg shook. Rocco reached for my spear gun.

"Gun not too big," the chief commented, examining my single sling aluminum arbolette with skepticism.

"It will do," I said, angry with him as I took the gun. "The bigger spears are hard to carry on planes."

I stood up on the center board and tried to collect myself. Holding the face plate of my mask tightly, I jumped backward into the sea. As always, on the first dive my body was shocked into a heightened state of awareness by the flow of adrenaline. I jackknifed downward to about twenty feet, clearing my ears on the way.

At once, I was in a different world. It was quieter out of the wind and turbulence of the open sea. After clearing my mask, I saw dozens of tropical butterfly, tang, and trigger fish darting around me. During my descent, I angled toward the rock face, parts of which were encrusted in coral. Shafts of iridescent light bounced off the rough edges of the projections. I realized that while the rock appeared to be a single shaft at the top, below the surface it widened like a pyramid with a series of caves at various levels. I saw the flowing green tail of a large parrot fish disappearing into the gloom of the nearest hole. Rocco was right; there were good-sized fish here. Yet the cave openings looked forbidding with the possibility they contained octopus or bad-tempered moray eels. It was easy for a free diver without scuba tanks to get snared in underwater caves and run out of breath.

I turned upward from the dive and broke the surface. To my dismay, I saw the boat had moved off quite a distance from me. After my second dive it was almost out of sight.

"Goddam!" I shouted. I couldn't believe it! They were just leaving me out here. An ominous feeling crept over me which I shook off, trying to relax. I convinced myself the chief had decided to troll in the general area while I worked the rock for fish.

I continued to dive for a while, trying to get into range for a shot at one of the large spotted sea bass feeding around the rock. They spooked easily and I didn't want to chase them down below thirty feet since I was out of condition, which meant a reduction in my usual capacity to hold air underwater. Moreover, I soon realized it would be plain stupid to spear any fish with no boat around. Sharks in the South Pacific have a reputation of picking up blood scents from long distances. I decided to glide along the edges of the upper rock holes and enjoy the dazzling ballet of tropical fish. There was an acute feeling of exhilaration within me that I had not felt in a long while.

Time got away from me as the sun, curving toward its zenith, poked through the clouds at last. Despite this, I was getting cold, tired, and hungry. To conserve energy, I decided to stop diving and hold on to a rock projection at one end of the spire. Soon I started to shake from the lack of body heat. I was also mad as hell.

"You son of a bitch—where are you?" I yelled in frustration toward the last place I had seen the boat.

The sea was growing more choppy with a rising breeze and the surge of the waves around the rock continually slapped my body against the sharp volcanic edges. I swam around the rock slowly trying to discover a section flat enough to climb up and rest. Finally, I found a small ledge, but it was slippery and there were rock spikes everywhere. I couldn't get a decent hold to haul myself up before a powerful surge of water slammed me against a wicked spur, gouging my left leg. The cut didn't appear to be too severe, but I couldn't stop the bleeding.

While my leg throbbed, I scanned the horizon and saw nothing. Suddenly, at the other end of the rock mass, there was a flash of movement. Turning quickly, I caught the shadow of a gray dorsal fin slicing through the water. With fear rising inside me, I squirmed against the rock trying to cock my spear gun. The shark made one long pass paralleling my position and then turned abruptly in one fluid motion and began accelerating straight toward me.

My gun was cocked and I could take the chance of trying to stop the shark with one shot at close range, or make the safer choice and get out of the water. I tossed my gun on a rock projection and then kicked hard upward with my fins and lunged over the jagged rocks onto the wet ledge. The pain was instant and terrible. As I draped my body on the rock, I found sawtooth cuts all over my chest and legs. Shifting to my side against the back of the ledge, I watched the shark race around in a frenzy from the blood trickling into the water below me. I reached for my gun and when the shark closed again, I fired. My body was shivering so much from the panic and cold that the metal shaft went wide, only grazing the shark's tough skin. I almost lost my balance and the gun fell out of my hands, clattering down the rock into the sea.

In the afternoon the sun came out more strongly and burned my salted wounds. The shark circled around the rock, its black eyes lifeless, waiting. Sometimes it would be out of my line of sight for a while and I would think it was gone. Then I would see that fin gliding through the water again. I estimated that it had been over three hours since the boat had left. While the sea swells washed over me at regular intervals, I knew I was growing weaker because it became harder to stay on the slippery ledge. My mind grew more detached and I felt as if I was in a state of suspension.

Was I supposed to die in this way? Maybe it was for the best, because without Sara I wasn't really living. I had always loved and respected the sea, and possibly I had come to this place to be released. It dawned on me that maybe it was no accident that I was going to die here, so why bother to resist? She came to me then—dressed in a white robe, hovering over my body, smiling. Her thoughts, gentle and probing, enveloped my mind. "Do not give up, Mark," she said. "Why not?" I asked her. "Then I could be with you." I felt her energy touch my face. "I wish you to take your life back, my love," she said. "I want you to live and be enriched by a full life for both of us. I am not dead and I will be waiting for you at the proper time."

Sara did not stay long, but while her spirit was with me it was as if she had the ability to release my soul from bondage within the anguish of my body. I felt empowered by my immortal self as the master over the desolate figure I saw lying on the rock. Moreover, my real self was in control of the mental despair of that physical mind that believed Sara was lost forever. Knowing she was here gave me the will to live. I had a choice of surviving by becoming strong, or giving up. With the help of Sara's spirit I returned to my body to continue the struggle. As I regained consciousness, I found myself sliding into the sea, yet I no longer felt powerless. While I started to pull myself up higher on the rock, I saw the shark driving toward me and I prepared to fight him with my knife.

There was a shout. Within seconds, the prow of Rocco's boat wheeled in alongside the rock between my perch and the shark. Fully alert, I saw the chief grab an oar and yell something which sounded like a battle cry. He jumped into the sea and I heard a loud splash and beating of water as he jammed the oar into the mouth of the shark. My god, the man looked magnificent!

I found myself being roughly hauled into the boat by the other two men, and a moment later Rocco hoisted himself over the stern, his wet, muscular arms the color of polished mahogany. As the engine rumbled into full throttle, the shark moved off with pieces of the oar he had chewed up sticking out of his mouth. We pulled away from the rock and Rocco took a seat across from me.

"Where fish?" he asked, breathing rapidly.

"What the hell are you talking about?" I said.

"No big fish?" the chief persisted.

"Listen, you fool," I cried, "you leave me out here alone for hours with the sharks and then when I'm half-dead, you ask why I don't have any fish!"

The chief rose to go to the other end of the boat.

"Good fisherman get mad when they bring no food home," Rocco answered me in a dignified manner. "I no catch anything either. Maybe we stay out too long in wrong places—eh?" His dark face was etched with resignation as he added that the village would not have a variety of large, delicious fish tonight because he had been unsuccessful.

As the great stone behind us receded, I came to the conclusion that it was not malevolence of any sort which caused Rocco to leave me stranded for hours, but the result of a singular mind. The chief had been preoccupied with the idea of his loss of status should I have bagged a large fish at the rock when he came home empty handed.

I pulled out my kit and dried off with a towel, gingerly dabbing at the cuts that had clotted. The sea became less choppy on the return trip home and I was able to eat another hard-boiled egg, the mango and a little bread. A strange calmness came over me. As I watched the chief staring majestically out to sea, I perceived there was an aura of nobility about him. I owed Rocco a debt of gratitude for providing me with a wake-up call to return to life again. Everyone seemed contained in their own thoughts until the island came into view.

"Chief, before we reach the pier, I want to thank you for jumping in the water to save my life," I said.

Rocco looked at me with a broad, toothy grin. Taking a coconut from the floor boards, he lopped off the end with a small hand ax and handed me the husk filled with the sweet milky juice.

"You good man—drink!" Rocco said, expansively, clapping me on the back.

The natives all laughed in a spirit of fellowship, and I felt united with them in their joy at simply being alive.

Crossing

THE QUARTER MOON CAST a pale silver glow across the ship's stern. It was a warm night in June and Alex had purposely made his way past groups of carefree passengers towards the solitude of the rear deck. He saw the woman once again standing at the railing. She was totally absorbed with the ocean, oblivious of him. As before, Alex was captivated by his vision of her illuminated in the moonlight. While he stood in the shadows away from the railing, Alex became aware of the churning of water from the ship's props. Raising his eyes beyond the woman, he noticed the narrow wake of white foam stretched out as a veil on the dark sea.

Alex had seen her at the same place yesterday on their first night out of New York, watching her for only a few moments, not wanting to intrude upon her mood. Alex was too uncertain then to do anything more than back away from her position at the railing. This evening he had returned, deliberately. There was a presence about the woman which possessed him as he watched her standing alone in this secluded area of the ship. Her clothing was odd; it seemed to Alex that the woman was wearing a headdress of some sort. He observed the folds of her garments were windshipped closely around a tall, thin figure. He imagined that the steady tail wind was pushing the French liner *Liberté* more rapidly toward his destination at the channel port of Le Havre.

His patience gone, Alex approached the railing at last. The woman turned and looked at him and he saw that she was a nun. Reacting to this deterrent, Alex felt a twinge in the pit of his stomach. She smiled at him and he was at once disarmed by her intelligent dark eyes and a face that was both gentle and resolute. Taking in the loose headdress which framed the nun's delicate features, once more Alex had a fleeting sense of regret. This is ridiculous, we're strangers, he admonished himself. He opened his mouth but no words came. Feeling awkward, Alex removed his cap and nodded respectfully. What am I doing? he thought desperately. Suddenly, he wanted to retreat, to get away and seek out the noisy activity of other passengers gathered around the main promenade deck.

"Is it not a beautiful night, Monsieur?" She spoke in French, her voice held a softness that unnerved him further. A moment later her dark eyelashes dropped allowing Alex to feel more in control and he wondered if she was uncomfortable with his intrusion.

"I...I'm sorry, sister," he said finally, "but my French is rather deficient." Now it was settled, he told himself. Since I am unable to converse with her I'll be able to leave gracefully.

"Oh, you are an American, then?" she said in a charming tone of accented English which sounded musical to him.

"Yes, but I plan to study French in Paris for a semester...for more proficiency," he volunteered lamely.

"Ah," she laughed easily, "then you will soon be out of the woods with our language." The nun's unaffected manner was disarming.

"I expect so," he responded, his nervousness making him more serious. Her luminous dark eyes, full of mirth, caused him to laugh and relax with her.

In that instant each perceptively realized they were drawn to the other. Alex moved closer and this was a mistake. Her expression changed and he saw her pleasure subside. He imagined the nun was withdrawing inside herself while smoothing out the folds of her clothes in a defensive gesture. Alex knew she wanted to break the spell between them. She is preparing to leave, he thought, not wanting this to happen. Alex looked at the lovely dark girl with milk-colored skin and forced himself into an air of detachment while edging back from her a little.

"Are you in training at an order in France or the United States?" he ventured, as if interviewing her for a job. Anything to detain her.

Her eyes flicked upwards at him with interest. "Well, as you can tell, I *am* a Frenchwoman—but why do you assume I am a postulant?" She was again smiling at him.

"Just a guess," he said with a trace of confusion. "Perhaps because you are not wearing the traditional black habit." Alex did not add that he also thought she might be too young.

"We are a hospital order—lots of white," she said, laughing at him.

"Oh," he answered dully.

Alex was unsure about her status; the permanence of a nun being in a religious order and involved in hospital work at the same time. What were the implications for her future? It was hard to think clearly while he stared at her.

"As it happens," she offered with no self-consciousness, "you are right, I am still in training."

"You have not taken final vows, then?" Alex spoke too quickly, his voice unnaturally high.

"Not quite yet," she replied abruptly, turning away from him. "I must go below. I have a companion traveling with me who has been seasick since we left New York."

Alex knew he had put her off again. "I'm sorry," he exclaimed. "Is there anything I can get for her?"

What a dumb thing to say, he thought. She's in a hospital order, for God's sake. Alex followed after her blindly, narrowly missing a deck chair.

"Thank you, no," she said to him. "Sister Marguerite is rather old and does not travel well."

"Are there just the two of you?" he asked, trying to be casual, feeling he was making things worse, yet not wanting their conversation to end.

The nun stopped and glanced at him. "Yes, usually when we travel. It is good rule, don't you think?"

This was more a statement than a question and Alex saw her cheeks turn pink. The flushing heightened her freshness for him, numbing his sensibilities further.

The girl turned away again and started down a steep passageway with a rustling of linen. In a second she would be gone. What else could he say to her? Anyway, what was the use of tormenting himself further by pursuing the unobtainable?

They reached the bottom of the stairwell. Involuntarily, Alex extended his arm to steady her, to touch her, then he pulled back realizing this was the wrong thing to do.

"Will I see you again?" he blurted out with sudden intensity. "That is, do you come out on deck occasionally for exercise?" His words were halting, metallic, so he made an effort to give her a relaxed smile.

The nun looked up, searching his open face. She seemed to be debating with herself while the warmth from the lower decks enveloped them.

"I try to, in the early evening when the sister is resting," she said at last, her eyes darkening.

The woman left him, her garments sliding off the stair landing while she descended further to the cabins below the main deck. His mind raced. Should he follow her? How absurd! What was wrong with him?

Alex did not know what to do with himself. He wandered back up to the belching smoke stacks of the ship and past a cluster of lifeboats. He thought about his past relationships with women and the fact that he never had found anyone with whom he wanted to form a deep attachment. In college and the army his male friends had made many temporary commitments to different women but this was not his style. Except for his mother and sister he had never felt devoted to anyone.

After finishing college during the Korean War, Alex was drafted into the army. He had only recently been discharged. He thought about his motivations for this trip to France. In college Alex had majored in international relations and he had decided to study at the Sorbonne for six months and become more proficient in French. He was at a crossroads in his life and unsure about the future and this troubled him. He felt alone, non-directed and empty.

As Alex made his way down another passageway to the bar, he tried to sort out what was going on in his head about meeting her. His emotions toward the nun baffled him. He considered the inaccessibility of her calling. Was that it? No, Alex reasoned with himself, it was just her. Perhaps it was the hidden quality about her demeanor that attracted him. He didn't really know, except whatever it was that had possessed his imagination had now turned to melancholy.

Alex took his drink into a dining area which had been converted to accommodate dancing and sat down at a small table.

People were pairing off and having a good time. He was soon dancing with a friendly girl who wore too much makeup.

"Where ya from?" she asked brightly.

"Oh, near Chicago," he said.

"Pleasure trip?"

"Sort of," Alex replied vaguely.

The girl danced well, her perfume overpowering his nostrils. Alex took pleasure in holding her tightly, venting his frustrations, but he wasn't truly flowing with her or the music. The dance number ended and he took the girl back to her table where her friends were laughing and joking with each other. They all looked at Alex expecting him to join them. Thanking her, he excused himself, wanting to get away from the crowded room.

He walked the open decks for hours, letting the cold spray of the Atlantic hit his face. At last he made his way to his own room and fell into the bunk with his clothes on, eventually dropping into a fitful sleep.

The third day of the transatlantic crossing dragged by and Alex grew even more restless. Although he feverishly patrolled the ship's decks for half the night trying to find her, his searching was fruitless. He lost his appetite while feelings of dejection which were new to him took hold. Why hadn't she kept her promise to return, he thought bitterly.

On the fourth day, sick from anticipation and disappointment, Alex was seeing vague images of her everywhere. At dusk, he ran into a large metal stanchion, banging his forehead, because he imagined seeing her a short distance beyond near a ladder leading to an upper deck. As he roamed about, some of the strolling passengers regarded him queerly while he pushed past them. He didn't care. Stewards offered tea and refreshments, inquiring if they could be of assistance. They were unwanted distractions. Alex was exhausted. He realized he had to end this madness.

Finally, after nightfall, Alex saw her again standing in the same place as before. The bell for the first dinner sitting had sounded and this part of the deck was deserted. He started to run toward her along the surging wooden planks of the ship. The troughs of the waves had become steeper as the voyage passed the three-quarter mark. The deck was wet and Alex slipped and fell. Picking himself up he paused and breathing deeply, tried to collect himself. Stiffly, he edged closer to her at the railing. Was this another apparition, another mistake? Alex noticed her clothing had changed. She was dressed in a black skirt with a heavy matching wool coat and hood.

"Hello," she said softly.

"Where have you been?" He spoke breathlessly, as if they had arranged some sort of appointment at this time and place.

She avoided his eyes and gazed at the rolling sea, not answering him.

"I've been looking for you. I wanted to…"

"I know," she said simply, as if listening to the sea.

"You haven't told me your name," Alex said, introducing himself.

"Sister Celeste," she answered gently.

"It suits you," Alex said, relaxing a bit.

The nun still looked out at the ocean, not responding to him.

"Is your companion still ill?" Alex didn't care what he was saying anymore. He had been through too much since their last meeting to feel cautious.

"She is better. I expect she will be up and about tomorrow."

"That's good," Alex said, not happy with this news. "You are partners, then?"

"Sister Marguerite and I were sent to New York for a specialized course in new surgical nursing techniques and she is worn out."

"You must be a very competent nurse. How long was the training in New York?"

"A year. I will finish my medical certification in France for full qualification," she said with pride.

"Does this mean your religious preparation—for the order I mean—is about over too?" His tone was rueful.

She turned toward Alex and gazed at him, searching his face. Her expression had changed and was more compelling.

"Yes—in December—I will take my place fully in the order as a hospital sister."

"Your final vows?" Alex spoke in a flat voice. His hands nervously rubbed the railing in a gesture she did not miss.

"Yes...in December..." There was something qualified about the offering of this information which stirred him.

"You are...not yet sure?" Alex said with presumption.

"There are those of us who have not been in the order all that long who have internal questions—doubts about our capacity for sacrifice—as the time draws near for our total acceptance within the order. We ask ourselves if we are adequate for the selfless dedication expected of us. There is honor in this work. You can see that, Alex?"

It was the first time she had spoken his name. The way she said it and the acknowledgment that she was taking him into her confidence allowed Alex to give these things greater weight than her declaration of a religious commitment.

Alex was composed again and he began to talk to her of his past and his original aspirations which had been on hold since his army discharge. He told her about his family and home. She spoke to him about her life in France, the regimentation for order novitiates and her desire eventually to be assigned to a hospital for the poor.

"I feel as though I have known you forever, as if we have been reunited after a long absence," Alex boldly told her, thinking how gracefully she was balanced against the railing while the ship moved up and down with the rolling waves.

She turned and looked at him, blushing.

Alex heard the Atlantic slapping the sides of the creaking liner and his ears hummed from a singing wind, making him lightheaded.

"Celeste," he said, dropping the Sister—as if this omission would make her proper name go away—"could there be any hope for...us?" Alex took her small hand in both of his.

"I am a nun," she said, holding her hand still.

"Not completely—just yet. And, you were a woman first."

"I have pledged myself to the church." Her tone was more introspective than blunt yet she withdrew her hand from his grasp. A gust of wind blew back the hood of her coat and with a gesture Alex found quite feminine, she tucked a few loose strands of short hair behind her ears.

"But there is still time…"

"Time for what?" she said with sudden intensity. "To destroy what I have worked so hard for—to bring sorrow to those who have placed their trust and faith in me."

"Words!" he exclaimed indignantly. "Celeste, other people's expectations are…other people are not going to live your life. Is there no justification for your existence except being a nun—no other form of life for you but this?"

She twisted away from the railing, directly facing him.

"Oh, it is so easy for you to say this because you do not see temptation as I do—giving in to desires of the body. What do you know of sacrifice, of dedication to a cause?"

Alex saw her eyes fill with tears and she turned her head away from him. He was silent.

"I am sorry, Alex," she said, her voice shaking. "I didn't mean to say that. I am arguing more with myself than you."

He could hold back no longer. Impulsively, he reached out for Celeste and taking her firmly by the waist pulled her close to him. She stopped shaking and her body responded. Alex cupped her wet face with his other hand and kissed her. For a moment her lips were soft against his, and then they grew cold. She stiffened and he released her.

The fire within him lessened. The return of his sensibilities brought sadness because Alex believed his aggressive act had hurt her.

"Celeste—forgive me," he said clumsily, "for taking unfair advantage of you. I had no right to do that."

"Please, Alex, I am not a fragile butterfly," she flashed at him, dabbing her face with a tissue. "I am more to blame than you. I have no regrets—and because of this I am frightened."

"Don't be, Celeste. It's no accident we have connected with each other. It is so good between us. You know this. I can't just let you go out of my life."

When the nun answered him, it was as if she were already a long way off.

"The decision for my life at Santa Teresa is to be made at noon services the day before Christmas. In that hour, all novices who are scheduled to take final vows may leave the order with compassion and understanding. If I remain after that hour—and do not walk through the gates of the convent—for me it will be forever."

"Why December 24th?"

"It is our custom. Traditionally, this is done once a year when a new class of novices become qualified for full membership in the order. The ceremony takes place on Christmas Eve."

"Can I visit you before...?"

"It is not permitted."

"At least tell me where Santa Teresa is located so I can wait for you on that date."

"About thirty miles south of Orleans. You must let me go now, alone. Please, Alex," she said decisively.

Alex took her hand again, his expression pleading.

"Celeste, I've fallen in love with you."

Her translucent, intelligent eyes filled with tears once again, her words soothing.

"I ask that you stay here. Late tomorrow, Sister Marguerite and I will depart the ship at its first stop in Cherbourg. Please do not…"

"I understand, Celeste."

"Goodbye, Alex," she said, lightly brushing his cheek with her fingers.

In December, Alex was on the southbound train out of Paris to Orleans. The next day, Christmas Eve, he arrived at the edge of the grounds of St. Teresa and waited at a place near the outer gate. It was snowing lightly but Alex was too feverish to feel the cold. His excitement was mixed with foreboding. Would she come? Dare he hope that the time he spent with Celeste on the ship was enough to change her mind? Did she care enough about him? He didn't know. His language studies in Paris had ended ten days ago, and finally the months of waiting were over.

Alex checked his watch. It was almost noon and his anxiety rose as he walked back and forth, crunching the snow next to the old wrought iron gates in front of him. He pictured Celeste's oval face in his mind, her dark hair tousled by the wind. He thought of her dancing eyes, the way she looked at him. Alex imagined this woman represented the purity of an ideal which he would never find again.

The bells began to toll the noon hour, their echo mournful in the frosted air. Alex held his breath and waited. The gates did not open. The snow soon began to fall harder. He approached slowly and fingered the large rust-covered lock and the handles joining the two gates together. He looked inside the courtyard beyond the gates and saw no one.

Long after the toll of the twelfth bell had died out, Alex kept his station at the gates of the convent. Finally, numb with cold, he walked slowly away, feeling emotionally drained. Had he only been infatuated with the unobtainable? The ache inside him told him, no. However fleeting, what happened on the ship was real enough and therefore it must have purpose. Alex then considered that his memory of what was possible in love would sustain him and somehow make him better for having loved Celeste. In a strange way, her decision brought resolution and an element of peace within him at last. All he had to do was get beyond tomorrow.

Lost in Time

THE WRATHFUL SAHARAN SUN bore down on Peter Ordway with a vengeance. After five days of marching by night and trying to sleep under a cut-out section of his parachute during the torrid, sluggish denseness of the hours between late morning and early evening, Peter hoped the merciful release of death would come soon. The endless walking on scorched earth had now become more of a crawl. His bloodshot eyes were caked with sand, making it difficult to see. During the first three nights he had tried to keep Polaris, which was low on the horizon, over his left shoulder. It was easier when he lined up this star with the overhead light from blue-white Vega in order to continue heading east where he imagined the pipeline was located. Last night, while stumbling onward, he had given up trying to concentrate on this task.

Peter had lost his bearings flying into the sandstorm. He thought he was in Algeria when, in fact, the blinding wind had carried his plane more than a hundred miles off course into Libya, so that he was now continuing to head in the wrong direction deeper into the Libyan desert. Utterly exhausted in this trackless world with no landmarks, the pilot had lost his concept for space and distance. He was aware of the passage of time only in terms of light and darkness.

Peter had finally come to the top of a low ridge with two large boulders close together and draped the remains of his parachute over them. Crawling under this makeshift tent, he braced himself against one of the smooth sandstone rocks. The water from his one-gallon canteen, rationed so carefully, had given out the previous night. Looking out over the wavy blur of a sloping sand ridge below him, the flyer decided it was useless to try to go further. Peter's tongue was swollen, his parched throat ached for liquid. With an air of abstraction, he picked up a handful of sand and watched the grains pour through his fingers, imagining he had created a beautiful waterfall fit for drinking.

To the pilot, the Sahara was a menacing territory of hard rocky flatland, dunes and wadies—ancient watercourses that had become dry river beds. He thought of flying over the mountain ranges of the Atlas, Hoggar and Tassili Plateau region where he could rise thousands of feet and within a short time drop into rolling desert plains of scrub and sand. Peter had always measured his domain from the air. As a pilot for American-Saharan Petroleum he was generally assigned flight routes over three countries: Morocco, Tunisia, and Algeria. On rare occasions, he would land in Tripoli or Benghazzi along the coast of Libya, but not often. Right now his home base was in Algiers.

Within the boundaries of Peter's usual flight paths—where the Sahara and the Great Western desert join as one against the recklessness of men—stretched three million square miles of blowing sand, harsh rock and the denuded wastes of burned earth. The challenge was oil. As his mind drifted in and out of consciousness, Peter thought about how he had trespassed once too often into this alien land.

He had been trained to fly cargo planes for the Air Force in the years between Korea and Vietnam. He decided to leave the service at the end of his enlistment for more lucrative private flying and greater personal freedom. For the last seven years American-Saharan Oil had paid him well to fly over hostile terrain in conditions which involved risk. Peter had almost left the company twice in the last year but he hadn't really considered where he would go next or what he could do other than flying.

Six days ago, Peter had taken a twin-engine Beechcraft on a 275 mile flight path from Gabes in Tunisia down to Ghadames to drop off assorted drill bits. Then he had picked up a few boxes of delicate geological instruments for the final leg of the flight farther south to the dirt air strip at Edjeleh. He hadn't needed a heavier aircraft for this trip and from the air he easily followed the oil pipeline along the Algerian-Libyan border toward Edjeleh. Since 1956, a light, high-grade petroleum had been produced in this district which was sent up to the coast of Tunisia.

After an hour the trouble started. Peter ran into the dreaded Cheheli, a sudden sandstorm so fierce he was unable to power his highly maneuverable light plane above the turbulence. The plane's crackling radio responded poorly to the storm and then gave out completely. The Beech rattled and strained for fifteen more minutes and Peter felt like its metal skin was being wrenched apart. Grinding sand blew into the engine cowling and induction system. From his gyrating compass, Peter knew he was all over the sky and way off course. The wind gusts reached eighty miles per hour. The port engine failed and the plane pitched downward in a spiral. The pilot fought the controls while his second engine sputtered and briefly he was able to flatten out his angle of descent. At 1,800 feet the plane stalled.

Peter snapped off the seat belt and tightened his parachute harness. Grabbing a canteen from the passenger seat, he looped the strap over his shoulder, forced open the door of the plane and jumped into space. Tumbling into the howling wind, Peter smashed against the side of his buffeting plane and almost blacked out. Holding himself in a ball, he had the presence of mind not to pull the ripcord until he thought he was near 1,000 feet. His chute opened but the ground came up hard and unexpectedly. Hurt and dazed he wrapped himself up in the parachute for hours until the end of the storm. Peter remembered that he had never heard the crash of his plane.

As he sat between the two boulders, Peter reached inside his loose-fitting khaki flight suit and gently rubbed his side. He was sure that hitting the side of the plane during the jump had cracked a rib and perhaps dislocated his left arm. After five days his body still ached. Laughing to himself, the pilot considered that his whole body was in pain so what the hell was the difference. The effort of any movement in his refuge was too great to bother about anyway.

Peter drifted in and out of delirium. He was aware only of being in bright fire which turned into a chilled blackness and then fire again. Once, he regained consciousness in the middle of the night and could see Claire as a vision in front of the rocks. She was just standing there looking at him. The vision was a recreation of their last meeting a week before he had left for Tunis on this assignment. Then, she spoke.

"Peter, you are thirty-six years old. How much longer do you want to live like a will-of-the-wisp?"

In his vision, Peter only heard Claire talking without any response from himself. Claire was a fair British girl with a wide, expressive face and a way of looking at him that reached inside his soul. Peter found her both winsome and sensible.

Clair's attraction for him lay in her humor, savvy and tenacity. Never concerned about trifles, Claire was grounded in the present. She always did what was expected of her as an employee for British Petroleum. At first, Peter thought their differences made for a good match. Now he wasn't so sure. He was a wanderer, looking for something—he didn't know what—that would truly make him happy, while her outlook on life was always clear and directed.

Peter listened to her again as he had on that last day.

"What are your dreams for our future. Do we have one? Look, Peter, I love you. I don't care what you want out of life as long as it is with me. All I ask for is some reassurance—some kind of commitment from you."

He couldn't remember how he had responded to Claire, so he just listened as she continued to talk to him at the edge of darkness near the boulders.

"Your thoughts are hidden, distant, and I wonder if I know the real you. You're maddening, because I never know what to expect from one trip to the next. Sometimes when you come home you're so remote it's as if we are starting all over again. I think it's best for me not to see you anymore, Peter, because it hurts so much to be off-balance and not know where I stand. Frankly, I'm not sure if you really want me anyway."

From under his parachute, Peter sadly looked out into the night. He watched Claire disappear into the darkness just as she had done on the streets of Algiers. He thought about how much he cared for Claire, yet he had not stopped her. His usual reaction to intense personal conflicts with women was to try to remain aloof and stay in control of his emotions. After the vision of Claire had gone, Peter still seemed unable to sort out who he was and where he had wanted to go. Now that he was dying, he wanted to find an anchor within himself, but it wasn't there. No answers came from the night. It really doesn't matter anymore, he whispered out loud, because this is where my life is going to end. Goodbye, Claire. Soon the pilot slipped into dreamless unconsciousness once more.

From a long way off, Peter felt rough hands shaking his body. Water was being poured down his throat and a hollow voice reached him from a great distance. He tried to swallow and choked from the gritty sand in his mouth. His face, chafed raw by the sun, received a snapping jolt and Peter opened his burned eyes a little. He saw a dark human apparition that contrasted sharply with the brilliant white sand. Feebly, Peter tried to fend off the phantom so he could go peacefully back to sleep. The pilot was lifted up, carried to a kneeling camel and rolled sideways onto a saddle. A rope secured his body and Peter was only aware of a swaying motion before the fog of unconsciousness was upon him again.

For days Peter's sleep was interrupted by water in his mouth and his face being washed by a formless presence. He had no perception of time, only background noises. At last he came awake, pulled a wet cloth from his eyes and looked around. He was in a leather tent propped up on a couch of rugs. The musky smell of burning tallow permeated the room. Peter's vision cleared and he drank from a gourd of water by his bed. His body was painfully sore, but he sat up and peered outside through an opened flap of his tent. Although it was evening, Peter could make out the tents of a desert camp behind a flickering campfire.

"Hey! Who's out there?" he cried hoarsely.

This brought an immediate response from the camp. There were running feet, voices, and moments later two black-robed figures ducked into the doorway in front of Peter's bed. They wore long, dark blue cloths wound around their heads and faces. Peter recognized them as Berber nomads. He tried to pull himself up and fell back on the rugs. One of the men turned around and barked a command. After a few minutes a boy brought in a warm plate of onions, dried dates and couscous which Peter began to eat slowly with his fingers. He thanked the men in Arabic and one of them nodded. It was difficult to get much food into his stomach and Peter only finished half the plate, not touching a large slice of bread and goat cheese. Within a few minutes he was asleep again.

Peter awoke a second time at dawn, feeling much better. He took a long drink, finished the rest of his meal from the night before and gingerly stood up. One of the Berbers saw him edging toward the animal hide opening of the tent. Peter waved but he was too weak to do anything but return to his bed. Suddenly, he heard the sounds of someone walking purposely toward him.

The man who entered was not native to the desert. Peter judged him to be in his fifties. He was short, with a hard, compact build and graying-blondish hair cropped close against his mostly bald skull. As he came near to the couch, Peter noticed his visitor was dressed in an old, faded military uniform that had obviously been repaired a number of times with wide stitching. There was a German Iron Cross pinned to his left pocket. The

man stood over the couch regarding Peter with pale blue eyes
and an icy directness that fascinated the pilot. Placing his stub-
by fingers on his hips, he spoke to Peter in English with a clipped
German accent.

"Ah, so the dead return. You are fully awake after three days
in another world," he declared.

"Three days! Have I been out that long?"

"You are lucky to be alive at all, my friend, but perhaps not
so fortunate to be here. We were on patrol. I was scanning the
desert with my field glasses when I saw your parachute staked
out on a ridge."

"Where am I?" Peter asked, rubbing his sore eyes.

His question was ignored.

"Your eyes will be quite painful for a few more days. The desert
leaves its mark on intruders. After a man's water gives out, the
sun takes his eyes and then his mind—ha, ha. You look like a
fried lobster."

"Am I near Edjeleh?"

The man's facial muscles tightened. "Where is that?" he asked
abruptly.

"Algeria, of course," Peter answered. What the hell, Peter
thought. Doesn't the man know of the Saharan oil fields?

"Algeria! Oh no, my friend. I suppose there is no harm in
telling you that we are definitely in Libya."

"Good Lord, was I blown that far off course? Tell me how far
into Libya am I. Are we near a settlement where I can get word
to...?"

"Enough!" The man interrupted curtly. "I will ask the questions please, if you don't mind. Do you speak any Arabic or
French?"

"Yes, both to a certain extent," Peter answered cautiously. "But what does that have to do with…"

"Because," the man shot back, "my comrades in arms are Tuareg tribesmen who do not understand English."

"The Blue Men of the Sahara? Yes, I have heard of them," Peter responded.

"Good, then you must also know of their reputation as skilled desert warriors who have a long history of fighting your allies, the French. Now, let's get down to business. First, allow me to present myself. My name is Captain Ernst Lang, 21st Panzer Division, Afrika Korps."

The man drew himself to attention, his back ramrod straight. His eyes glittered in undisguised relish with this introduction.

Peter laughed. "What is this, some kind of joke? Who in the hell are you supposed to be?"

The German's bull neck puffed out. Angrily, his jaw moved from side to side in a grinding motion.

"I can assure you that your present situation is hardly a joking matter, Lieutenant. I must officially inform you that I am placing you under military arrest," he said, pulling down his ill-fitting tunic so it was briefly wrinkle-free.

"What are you saying, Lang?" Peter exclaimed loudly.

He felt light-headed from the effects of prolonged dehydration. He thought he might still be hallucinating.

"*Captain* Lang to you, Lieutenant Ordway." The German pulled out Peter's wallet from his coat pocket. "I have confiscated your identity papers—and knife, of course." He opened the wallet and read from Peter's expired reservist card. "Peter Ordway, First Lieutenant, United States Air Force—which I interpret to mean United States Army Air Corps."

"Not since 1947," Peter said, shaking his head in disbelief. "Does this mean you're masquerading as some kind of refugee turned rebel, getting your kicks out of threatening people lost in the desert? Goddammit, what's going on here?"

With effort, the German controlled himself by speaking methodically, as a schoolmaster instructing a new student.

"Lieutenant, I want you to listen carefully. I am a German tank officer. Your misfortune is that you, a downed Allied pilot on a military air reconnaissance mission, have allowed yourself to be captured. You are a prisoner-of-war under my authority. Really, what could be simpler? The only question which remains is, are you going to cooperate and make things easy for yourself, or be difficult?"

Peter's voice rang with fury as he stood up. "Reconnaissance pilot! Listen, you son of a bitch, let's get this straight, I work for an American oil company and..."

The German pushed Peter back down on the rugs and both were aware that a small group of Berbers had gathered outside the tent. Peter saw the German exhibit a defensive posture as if he might be worried about losing face.

"I would advise against any further outbursts," Lang said evenly. "You are only going to cause more unpleasantness. I will continue this interrogation later after you fully recover and are more rational. We are a small scouting party and have delayed our departure until you were able to ride back with us to our main camp. I will have Kondi bring you proper covering for the trip."

"Are we going in the direction of the oil fields where I can phone?" Peter barked.

The German was highly amused by this request.

"Lieutenant, I can assure you there are no telephones where you are going." With that he stalked out of the tent.

After a few minutes a teen-aged boy entered and gave Peter a white djellaba to throw over his own clothing. The robe was not a bad fit. He was also presented with five yards of darkly-dyed cotton for a turban which Kondi helped Peter wrap around his head and face. The young man stood back, admiring his handiwork and motioned Peter outside where he was given mint tea, dried millet and round cakes.

"Kondi, do you speak Arabic?" Peter inquired.

"A little," said the boy, who had been speaking Tamacheq, the Berber language of the Tuareg that Peter could not decipher.

The camp was breaking up and Peter saw eight men loading the tents and supplies onto the backs of kneeling camels. The Tuaregs were tall, light-brown men with elongated facial features, slender limbs and large eyes. All wore dark blue veils leaving only their eyes exposed. Peter had heard that the blue indigo dye of the veil could come off on their faces, which is why they were called the Blue Men. To Peter, there was an imposing air of mystery about them. The Tuaregs were distant and paid little attention to the American, which added to their effect on him.

Shortly, the German came over to where Peter was standing alone. The pilot saw he was wearing a black burnoose with a hood but no veil. He could not tell if Lang was wearing his old uniform underneath. The fact that Lang's military clothing was not in evidence seemed to Peter to be of significance because the German's demeanor was less confrontational than the night before.

He began speaking to Peter in a more relaxed conversational tone as if he were a tour guide. "Ordway, as I told you we are a scouting party, and because we are not a large caravan our food is limited. We will eat only skimpy meals twice a day. As you can see, our camels are largely *mehari*, a trotting camel used for long-distance travel. However, we do have a few *djemal* camels, the more coarse and slower pack animals. Thus, we won't be moving rapidly—which will be easier for you," he said condescendingly. "We will need at least a week to get back to our home base."

"And where is that?" Peter asked bluntly. "Are we going in the direction of the Algerian settlements?"

The German's face darkened. "That is no concern of yours," he snapped. "Strict discipline will be maintained. You and I are considered Europeans by these men, and so I do hope you will not disgrace our respective cultures by bad behavior."

"What the hell is that supposed to mean, Lang?"

"Captain Lang," the German remonstrated once again. "It means," he continued, "that you are to obey orders, just as I do. Tafik, a *madugu*—caravan master—is the man up front who is in command. The camels will travel single file and you will be directly in front of me because I am responsible for your conduct."

"Meaning what?"

"Meaning that escape is useless. If you were to try to run away—even if we let you go—you would only die in the desert. There are no settlements nearby, as you well know. We are in a no-man's land, Lieutenant. I expect you resign yourself to being a prisoner-of-war and be thankful you are alive. Now, do you know how to ride a camel?"

"I have ridden, but never for more than a few hours."

The German smiled wickedly. "Then you are in for a treat—ha, ha—a very sore backside, but you will learn as I did. Come, allow me to show you your camel," he said, leading Peter over to a particularly large beast who was pawing the ground and smacking his huge lips.

Peter recognized that Lang was outwardly more at ease while lecturing about desert life to a non-resident.

"Notice the Tuareg saddles are light, with small, circular seats that love to crush testicles. Ha, yes, you will learn. It is chair-backed with a cross-shaped pommel in front to hold on to so you can lean back and rock with the animal's motion. Keep your feet on the neck. We walk beside the camels for an hour or two each long day, which will give you some relief. Kondi is bringing over your goatskin water bag. I caution you to ration it carefully."

Peter wanted to ask more questions but decided it would be useless. Soon the party was underway in single file. As the ride began, Peter's shoulder and ribs felt better, which indicated they were bruised and not broken as he had feared. To Peter's dismay, the caravan of camels walked eastward, farther away from Algeria into unchanging emptiness. Swaying back and forth amid a world of endless sand, Peter listened to the dragging, pock-pock gait of his camel's enormous feet.

The days went by and Peter's discomfort from camel riding grew less as he became somewhat stronger. Lang had quieted down and, except for a few non-confrontational remarks to Peter about the camels and terrain, he appeared to be in an emotional lull. The German's primary interest was scanning the desert with an outdated pair of military binoculars. Peter's main contact with the camp was Kondi, who brought his meals in the morning and evening but did not want to answer questions. Peter found it curious he was not asked to join the Tuareg when they ate, which went against the usual hospitality of the desert. He suspected this decision had more to do with Lang than the nomads.

One evening Kondi brought Peter his food and told him they would reach the main camp the following day. An hour later Lang walked over to where Peter sat next to the bed roll he had been given. The German was wearing his uniform again. Although his manner was somewhat agitated, it was nonthreatening. He began to talk to Peter in an officious tone.

"Lieutenant Ordway, the men do not wish to treat you as an outcast, but since you are under my command until we reach camp, I thought it best to keep you in solitary, so to speak, until I am able to complete my interrogation."

This announcement made Peter angry. The days of fear and uncertainty after the crash had taken their toll.

"Listen, you insane bastard, stop calling me Lieutenant. I am a civilian employed by an American oil company. I inspect damaged pipelines, deliver equipment, pick up passengers going into or out of the oil fields. I..."

"Make military reconnaissance flights over enemy territory," the German broke in smugly.

"My services have nothing to do with local or national groups from a military or political standpoint. It's oil business. Why don't you contact the people at Edjeleh or the authorities in either Algeria or Libya? They'll verify the truth of what I'm telling you."

The German fingered his Iron Cross and then sighed deeply. He spoke in a voice filled with resignation.

"You know, Ordway, I am not an unreasonable man. I realize you have been under a strain, but you owe me a debt. It was I who found you and saved your life and all I ask in return is for you to make a clean breast of your spying activities before we report to Zohar, the camp commandant. Our commandant is also a reasonable man. I can assure you I am not without staff experience in the workings of Allied intelligence, but your cover story is so poorly fabricated that you insult my position as a combat field officer. Ach, do you think a Wehrmacht officer in the Afrika Korps cannot recognize an enemy pilot in U.S. Army flying clothes? How can you expect me to believe such lies?"

"You're wrong! I'm not lying, why would I lie?"

"To avoid internment as a captured American flyer, naturally. I have never heard of this Edjeleh. And these Saharan oil centers you speak of—we both know that all oil in this desert is imported."

"Imported! Where have you been since 1956?"

This unnerved the German, who nonetheless pressed on, his words tumbling forth with indignation as if released from an uncorked bottle.

"Lieutenant, I suspect you are attached to the American Second Armored Division which closed in on us with the British Eighth Army. Well, your deceptions won't work with me, Ordway! I'll have you know that as a member of the 21st Panzers, I escaped from your encirclement in Tunisia on the plains of Medenine."

"What in hell are you talking about?"

"I'll tell you what!" Lang cried shrilly. "I was there! We were down to eighteen fighting Tigers…"

"Tigers?"

"Tanks, you idiot," the German hissed, not appreciating the interruption. "Stop playing the fool with me. It is important you know just who you are up against. My sergeant, Hans—a brave fellow who died later from his wounds—and I broke out of your pincer movement at Wadi Akarit and escaped."

Lang stopped for a moment to catch his breath. His face squeezed tightly with internal conflict. Then, he plunged on.

"A pretty situation, eh? No aircraft support, shells whining around us, confusion—death. I broke out in the middle of the night, to find and assemble other units in our battalion, to fight again when the odds were more even. I was never captured, which is more than I can say for you, Ordway."

The German was so breathless that he had stopped talking. He began pacing back and forth in rapid, jerking movements, his hands tightly clasped below his spine. Lang was sweating, although the air was cool, and his bulging eyes had taken on a fanatical stare. The pilot saw that Lang was seeking personal recognition and acquiescence from him, but Peter was in no mood for passivity. He was aware the German was deranged and probably dangerous, yet at this moment Peter didn't care. He had a lot of pent-up rage himself over being bullied, and he was tired and impatient. Peter decided to feed into Lang's vanity and personal turmoil by egging him on to see where it might lead.

"Tell me," Peter spoke sharply, "when did you escape this Allied encirclement with your own tank?"

Peter saw another sudden change in the German. He stopped pacing and smiled inappropriately. Lang began to speak quietly, as if he were about to take the airman into his confidence as someone who would appreciate a military operation.

"The end of April, 1943. I decided it was time to give your boys another lesson in military tactics. The 21st was never where we were supposed to be, eh?"

The German laughed delightedly and then suddenly grew very serious. His face twitched repeatedly as he continued.

"There was talk of our surrender in a few days—not because of a lack of bravery by the Afrika Korps—or the absence of Field Marshall Rommel—or even the considerable fighting skill of your armies."

Lang was shouting now, the momentum of his account carrying him to new heights.

"Oh, no! No! Ordway, it was treachery—yes, betrayal of our battle plans by the the Italian High Command, our so-called Allies, the most inept soldiers I have ever had the misfortune to serve with."

"Mmm, so, you left the scene of the battle?"

"To fight another day, Ordway. There was never enough to eat, we were low on ammunition and fuel, most of our tank units decimated…," Lang explained defensively.

"And you have been out here in the desert for twenty-four years still fighting World War II like some desert Don Quixote jousting with windmills?"

Peter was on a roll now and it felt good to watch Lang's contorted face. It was not in his nature to be cruel, but he was tired of being pushed around unjustly.

"As I see it, the facts are these, Lang," Peter said, mocking the German's own clipped voice. "You ran from the front lines near the end of the fighting just when your men needed you most. This would be considered an act of cowardice in my army. You should have been court-martialed for desertion."

"Swine! You call me a coward!" Lang screamed. "A soldier decorated by General von Ravenstein himself!"

The German could contain his fury no longer and charged, his head low, catching Peter full in the stomach. Both men sprawled in the sand. Peter was up first and sent a vicious punch to the side of Lang's face. They fell to the ground again, grappling with each other while the German yelled and cursed, trying to get his fingers around Peter's throat. Peter found Lang too much to handle despite his own age advantage. He had not fully recovered from the crash and Lang was a powerful man in a frenzy of rage. Peter heard the shouts of the Tuareg and Lang was pulled off him. Tafik, their leader, ordered Kondi to take Peter away to the other side of camp for the rest of the night.

The caravan grew silent and Peter was left virtually alone except for Kondi, who indicated he should sleep. The next morning the young man was back with a light breakfast and stayed with Peter as the caravan prepared for their final day. Peter found he had been placed at the opposite end of the line of camels from Lang. Good riddance, he thought.

Six hours later, as they entered the main Tuareg camp, Peter had grown more fearful about his ultimate fate with these desert nomads. He really didn't know anything about them except that everyone had an assortment of rifles, swords, and knives. Peter felt they could hardly be considered pastoral traders. He considered his altercations with the militant Captain Lang and how the Tuareg apparently condoned the treatment he had received at the hands of the German soldier. If the main camp of these tribesmen supported Lang in the same way as the small caravan with Tafik at its head, they could easily decide he was too troublesome and get rid of him. He recognized this would be the expedient course of action. After all, Peter thought, of what use am I to these people?

Tafik pulled his camel alongside Peter. He was alert and composed, exuding a somber mantle of leadership which Peter found a pleasant contrast to the German's madness. From the time of their first meeting, Peter felt Tafik possessed a high degree of intelligence, but that did not mean he was sympathetic to Peter's cause.

"This is Camp Calle," Tafik said.

"Calle?"

"It means 'jewel' in Arabic. You will follow me to your quarters and stay there until I talk to our chief. Do not ask any more questions now."

Peter saw the Tuareg encampment was nestled between two tips of a crescent-shaped rock canyon. The nomads had arranged their large, circular, animal-hide tents, propped up by heavy wooden poles, around the canyon entrance where there was a large well. Peter noticed goats grazing nearby and he could make out clusters of date palms and signs of vegetation farther up the canyon.

While the caravan moved into the center of the oasis, Peter saw some thirty to forty men and women. Children scampered about the women, who were unveiled. Everyone stopped what they were doing and stared openly at Peter while he dismounted and was led away to a mud-clay block structure built against the cliff on one side of the canyon. Inside the dwelling it was a little cooler and Peter found a low wooden bedstead which could be easily broken down for transport. The bed had a mat of palm fiber and on the wall hung a water bag. There was a covered hole in the floor for the toilet.

Tafik told Peter he was not permitted to leave the room and after closing the door, he placed a wedge underneath to prevent it being opened from the inside. Peering out the small window, Peter could see one side of the rock canyon in exaggerated sharpness, a characteristic of the Sahara at this time of day. A few women were bringing water up in a bucket from the well, their white cotton robes gleaming in the twilight.

That night and all the next day Peter languished in his room. Kondi came twice to bring food and water, but he had obviously been told to say nothing. Swooping, bulbous flies continually tormented Peter while he tried to rest on the hard bed. His hands and bearded, sunburned face itched from the swollen bites of ravenous sand fleas he had encountered in the desert. Peter sweated, and between fitful naps in the oppressive heat, he drank his water and waited for someone to come for him. Strangely, he wasn't nervous anymore, he just wanted something to happen, good or bad.

Finally, at dusk, Tafik returned and told Peter to follow him out the door. They walked toward a prominent tent in the center of the camp. An imposing tribesman with two western-type bandoleers lined with rifle cartridges slung over his shoulder came out and went away. Tafik motioned Peter inside, where he saw an old man seated comfortably in a low, folding chair of polished wood. At his waist hung a curved dagger, beautifully inlaid with silver and with an ivory handle. Nearby, a Roman lamp, an earthenware dish with a wick floating in goat butter, held a low flame.

"This is Zohar, our chief and my father," Tafik said. "Father, I present the American flyer, Ordway."

"Bonjour, Ordway," the old man said in a soft undertone. "I understand you speak some French and Arabic, which will make our communications much easier, although I must tell you most of the inhabitants at Camp Calle understand only our dialect of Tamacheq. Let us begin with mint tea while you sit down and tell me about yourself."

Tafik motioned Peter to a place on a pile of rugs and, after pouring out three glasses of tea, positioned himself next to his father. Peter realized at once that he would be dealing with a shrewd, perceptive leader of men. He kept his remarks about himself brief and to the point, stressing that he was a civilian pilot on routine business for an American oil company and had crashed in a sandstorm.

Zohar nodded politely and asked Peter about his home base of operations, how long he had been working in North Africa, and his thoughts about the region.

After these preliminaries, Zohar came to his more immediate problem.

"Mr. Ordway, I hear from my son that you have had some difficulties with our Captain Lang."

"That's putting it mildly, sir," Peter answered. "The man is a psycho—he's crazy—he thinks we are still fighting World War II."

Zohar gave Peter a stoic smile and rubbed his bony hands against the hot glass of tea to warm them.

"Mr. Ordway, Captain Lang has a troubled mind. Our people love him, but we recognize he is possessed by a djinn, an unearthly spirit, whom he must serve. This demon even torments the captain in his dreams. In the middle of the night we have heard him cry out as if in the heat of battle. Occasionally, he wears his military clothes when he perceives there is a threat—a strategic need for his services. I want you to know that we have great respect for him, as he has been with us for many years. Captain Lang fought valiantly with us in our campaigns against the French."

"But the French Foreign Legion cleared out five or six years ago, around 1960, didn't they?" Peter asked.

The chief raised his hand patiently and closed his eyes in a sign for quiet from the American.

"All in due course, Mr. Ordway. Let me continue with the altercations between you and Captain Lang. We have had a conference with him and he has been told that from now on you are under my jurisdiction, which he has accepted. As a highly trained German soldier he respects my position and calls me the camp commander—or commandant—in his words. However, my proper title is *amrar,* which means tribal chief. I have told him you are to be treated with consideration as our guest."

"Well, that's an improvement," Peter said, "but am I also a prisoner of war?"

Zohar and his son exchanged meaningful glances.

"Mr. Ordway, let us say you are in our custody for a while. Now that I am fully aware of your situation, I will ask Captain Lang to deal with you as an equal, although he thinks of you as an opponent, to be sure. For my people, you and the captain are two Westerners, despite the fact you come from different countries. However, I wish you to know that we consider him to be a tribal member, while you are an outsider. In Captain Lang's mind, we are the only family he has left and he has made it clear he wishes never to leave us. He was trained as an engineer before the war. His talents are valuable in many areas, such as overseeing the depth and efficiency of our wells, for example. And yet, today he lives in his mind somewhere between our world of the desert and the great desert war he lived through years ago. Our land has become his home. On the other hand, Mr Ordway, you wish to go back to your people as soon as possible; am I correct?"

"You have that right," Peter exclaimed.

"Then I will strike a bargain with you. I want you to indulge Captain Lang with his conceptions for the remainder of your stay with us. This includes addressing him by his rank in the German Army. I would like you also to engage in a small charade and not continue to cause him further distress about the end of World War II and your country's victory—something he cannot accept. Do I make myself clear?"

"You want me to humor him, then."

"Yes, by whatever means necessary."

"To go along with the idea that the war is not over?"

"We are still fighting a war of sorts among ourselves in the Sahara, so you might think of that as an extension of World War II. Could you manage that, Mr. Ordway?"

"To save my skin, yes." Peter thought for a moment and then added, "Could I be rather ambiguous? Do it in my own way?"

"Certainly, but be careful. Captain Lang is clever," Zohar cautioned Peter with an accommodating smile. "Do not patronize him. I want our captain to be treated with respect."

"How much abuse must I take from him to stay in your good graces?"

"No physical abuse. Verbally, I cannot say, but it will be softened if you are able to admit to being a prisoner of war."

"Am I?" Peter asked again.

"Well, of a sort." Both Tafik and his father laughed.

"Can you carry this off, do you think?" Zohar continued.

"That's asking a lot. What do I get in return?"

Zohar grew stern. "Your life and a trip home eventually. However, I must be completely honest with you, Mr. Ordway, this will not happen for some months."

"Months!" Peter protested.

"Alas, yes. We cannot send out a special caravan hundreds of kilometers lasting weeks toward the settlements on a special trip just for you."

"I don't understand," Peter objected. "Your caravan was in the west when you found me."

"That was different. Our small party was in the Tinerhert Mountains checking encroachments and bartering on a major north-south trade route from Gabes through Ghadamas."

"What's different about it? Why can't you just take me back to Ghadamas?"

"We are a small tribe and have our priorities. For one thing, this is not a region where we plan a return."

"Where am I now?"

"That is something you do not need to know. We do not want the authorities to know the location of our sanctuary here. Our water is getting low, and we are preparing to move a long distance away from our current position. That is when we will take you to an area where you can get home."

"But why are you concerned about the authorities?"

Zohar and his son spoke rapidly to each other in Tamacheq. They appeared to come to a decision, and Zohar turned back to Peter.

"Libya under the current monarchy is pro-German and therefore anti-French, which makes all of us, including Captain Lang, particularly happy. Our original home was in the Hoggar Mountains of Algeria, and we fought the French colonialists there for many years. Our tribe is subservient to no one. We have enemies. Do you know the term *Fellagha*?"

"Yeah, in Algeria it means a rebel."

"Exactly. That's what we are here. My people are not ordinary Berbers, but Tuareg freedom fighters. Colonization by the French and then nationalization of our homeland took from our people the very things that made us kings of the desert."

"I'm still not sure how an old German army officer fits into all this," Peter said.

"When Captain Lang escaped from the Allies in Tunisia during the war, he joined a caravan of Jerban Berbers there, and they eventually brought him south to our group. We were glad to get someone of his abilities. He spoke a number of languages and knew the kind of military tactics useful to our own war."

"Fighting the French, you mean?"

"Yes, and others such as those pigs, the Shambas, our bitter enemies, who collaborated with the French Foreign Legion. Captain Lang is courageous and utterly loyal. He is a fierce combat soldier who refuses to give up regardless of the odds. Do you understand why I am telling you all this, Mr. Ordway?"

"Yes, sir. I get the picture," Peter sighed.

"I hope so, because my son tells me that you insulted our captain and called him a coward. Is that true?"

"Yeah, I was fed up. I wanted to get to him."

"Now that you comprehend his history with us and our position, I want you to apologize to Captain Lang for that remark. Will you do this?"

"I guess so," Peter said with resignation. "I have a love for freedom just as much as you do."

"Then we understand each other. My son has arranged for a return of your papers. Your own tent will be provided while you remain with us. We will respect your privacy as much as possible and expect you to do the same with the people of Camp Calle."

Zohar indicated the meeting was over. Tafik rose, bowed to his father, and led Peter out of the tent.

"Look, Tafik," Peter said despairingly as they walked away, "why can't I be taken out someplace where I can try to get home by myself. I'll buy one of your camels. Just give me a few provisions to help the odds a bit and let me go. Hell, I couldn't find your camp again even if I wanted to—which I don't."

"Mr. Ordway," Tafik replied in a dismissive tone, "you are not of the desert. You would never make it. I think my father's terms are fair considering the circumstances. For your own good, I advise you to exert caution among us and be patient. Say no more about this for the time being. Kondi has been instructed to attend to your needs."

Tafik led Peter across the camp to an isolated tent that had been prepared for him and then went away without further comment.

The next morning Peter left his tent to see if he could wander about and stretch his legs without being hindered. He noticed the Tuaregs were unhurried in their movements around the camp. Their lithe bodies appeared to sway, rather like the camels they rode, in a fluid motion as if they were walking underwater. Peter had heard that the Blue Men displayed a kind of methodical aimlessness to Westerners, but now that he was living among them, he felt this represented more of a silence of movement, similar to cats.

Strolling by the tents of the camp, Peter found that his keepers regarded him more with curiosity than suspicion, and he wondered if the nomads had accepted him on orders from Zohar. They seemed more comfortable by his presence this morning, and it was nice to watch the people at their daily chores. Peter saw women making *kesra*, the Tuareg bread, using coarse flour with water, kneading the dough into flat cakes, and placing them on coals of palm wood. Others were weaving, darning clothes, gathering water, and milking their goats. All the women were unveiled and most wore colorful head cloths. They regarded Peter with proud, steady eyes as he walked past and he nodded to them in polite acknowledgement.

Since no one stopped him, Peter continued on into the canyon and saw two boys up a palm tree picking dates while a small girl below carried off a palm frond they had tossed down.

Peter knew of the many uses of the desert palm, such as weaving the fibers into cord, making containers, and designing the fronds to keep blowing sand out of the tents. In many respects, Camp Calle was no different from other desert camps Peter had visited, except here there were no Muslim prayers five times a day, the women were boldly open, and all the men had swords and rifles.

As Peter strode up the canyon, he heard a clanging of steel. Rounding a turn, he saw Lang dueling with a young man. The German soldier wore a knee-length shirt tied in at the waist and baggy trousers tucked into his boots. Both men wore chest guards and eye protectors fashioned out of wood. Peter thought they looked like Japanese samurai swordsmen. Using the *takouba*, a long, straight double-edged sword, the German was obviously giving his young opponent a fencing lesson. After a few minutes with the *takouba*, Lang instructed that their dangerous weapons be set aside and replaced by *kendo*-type bamboo training sticks. There was an increased flurry of movement, and Lang roared with approval as the boy parried and thrust against his fencing master's defense. Peter stayed back out of their line of sight until they had finished.

The student left, and Lang stripped to the waist. He wiped sweat from his well-muscled body with a cloth as Peter came forward, encouraged that the German was out of uniform.

"That was very impressive, Captain Lang," he offered.

"From my university days at Heidelberg," the German replied coldly. "The Tuaregs prefer the sword over the gun with their enemies," he added ominously.

Lang continued to towel off casually, drawing out the moment, his pale blue eyes hard and unforgiving. Peter knew it was time to try and make peace with this man.

"Captain Lang, I have told your commander everything about my mission without revealing those secrets of war which I am honor bound to keep as a captured prisoner."

The German immediately stopped what he was doing. His head cocked to one side as he ran his tongue over his lips. Lang's arm and shoulder muscles tightened, then flexed with tension. However, his sinister demeanor had abruptly changed to one of expectation. Lang was a study of contrasts. Fascinated, Peter didn't know what to make of this behavior.

"Aha! So you admit to being a lieutenant in your Air Corps?" Lang said coarsely.

"Yes, that was my flight rank in the service," Peter answered truthfully.

"You mean, *is* your rank!" Lang corrected, his eyes darting from side to side.

Peter hesitated. "Yes," he answered, watching Lang's mannerisms carefully for further changes in mood.

"Lieutenant Ordway, how are things at the front…generally speaking of course?"

Peter took a deep breath and plunged in. "Well, Captain, as you know, under the terms of the Geneva Convention I am not required to reveal our tactical positions, but I think I can say that things have been quiet for a long time."

Lang's expression altered again. There was almost an imploring look about the German—a need for verification that confused Peter because it seemed out of character.

"Ah—the troops of both sides are tired, do you think?"

"Yes, Captain, that would be a fair assumption."

"But there are local skirmishes—the sort of action one would expect between great campaigns?"

"Yes, Captain Lang, the usual military strategy that you are most familiar with in the desert."

Peter was amazed that these vague responses seemed to satisfy the old soldier. Lang now shifted to a more compelling line of inquiry. He spoke in a low tone with traces of melancholy. The rapid transformations of behavior by the German caused Peter to stay alert with each response.

"Ordway, can you at least tell me how Germany fares…how is my country?"

"Your country is distinguished and prosperous, Captain."

"I am certain there still exists a sense of purpose among my people as they look at their conquests and plan for the continued greatness of the Fatherland."

Peter had to swallow hard to get that one down and he paused briefly. Before he had time to answer, the German continued on, his voice rising, the words sounding almost evangelical.

"You know, Lieutenant, we will never give up. We will fight on for our ideals."

"Yes, your people are very courageous—as you are, Captain."
Peter hesitated, trying to separate this soldier from the savage
regime of Nazi Germany he had heard so much about while growing up. "I want to apologize for my accusations about your last
tank campaign. Zohar has explained that I was quite wrong, but
I'm sure you know I spoke out of anger."

"I accept your apology, Ordway," the German said with grave
satisfaction. "I too was perhaps overzealous, but you are my first
captured American pilot."

"Oh...yes," was all Peter could muster up.

"Your countrymen are worthy adversaries," Lang went on
cheerfully, "and now that the war is over for you and you have
decided to be honest with us, I see no reason why we cannot be
civil to each other as two soldiers thrown together by the fortunes
of war. Zohar has asked for this on my part and I have been
informed he plans repatriation for you."

Lang put on his shirt and taking Peter by the arm in a father-
ly fashion, accompanied him out of the canyon. Peter felt awkward.
He found it difficult to match this impulsive man's attempts at
camaraderie. Lang's mercurial nature never lacked for surprises.
It dawned on Peter as they walked together that, while Lang seemed
deceptively compliant at the moment, he had caught a glimpse of
the German soldier's hidden burden of painful loneliness.

"You know, Ordway, I must confess, it is a pleasure for me to
have the company of someone from our part of the world."

"Yes, for me as well, it is good to be able to talk to someone in
English," Peter stammered awkwardly.

The German stopped abruptly, anticipation on his face.

"Tell me, Ordway, do you play chess?"

"Only tolerably, Captain Lang. I'm very rusty."

"Ah, ho ho! We will soon remedy that. I have carved a chess board and pieces out of palm wood. The Tuareg have a passion for board games. It will help pass the time for you. Military campaigns on the chess board—ha, yes! A tonic for both of us, don't you think?"

As the weeks passed, Peter's association with this exile from civilization took on new dimensions. They began calling each other by their first names during nightly chess games. Lang found instructing Peter in the nuances of chess far more enjoyable than beating him, and when Peter began to win more frequently, the German took full credit as his mentor. To the soldier, each piece on the board represented military units. The pawns were infantry, knights and bishops were tanks, and rooks became heavy artillery. Between games they would talk. In the beginning their conversations centered around the German's campaign memories.

"Ah, Peter," Lang said after a particularly difficult chess game, "these matches between us remind me of the cat and mouse strategy of the 21st Panzers. We were heady conquerors in the early days. Field Marshal Rommel, my idol, was still in command then. Ho! You should have seen me then. My body up high in an open tank turret—our eighty-eight-millimeter cannon booming —racing forward from one victory to another. Ach, yes, it was wonderful! We called ourselves the black knights of the desert, after the medieval knights of the Teutonic Order of Germany. Ho, Peter! You know armored units are considered calvary, just as a convoy of camels. Ha! But a knight of the air might not appreciate these fine distinctions."

Peter smiled. He had learned that Lang did not expect him to comment much during these reminiscences, because the German had disengaged mentally into the events of another time and did not like interruptions. He required an attentive audience and little else. Peter came to the conclusion that Lang's delusions about the present stemmed from the soldier's need to nurture and even protect his memories of the past. The pilot was reminded of Zohar's warnings about dealing with Lang. Believing that he was still an active, viable tank officer preserved Lang's identity since he was unable to accept the humiliation of surrender. Captain Lang was an obsessive fanatic, but there were times when he was calm and appeared to Peter to be rational and even ingratiating. The American resolved that if he wanted to survive, he had to learn to manage the duality of Lang's nature. The German lived in a fantasy world of World War II within the current reality of having a respected life among the Tuaregs. Peter found it was easier to deal with Lang when the topics of conversation did not include the war.

"Ernst, do you miss your family?" Peter asked one evening.

"Ach, I have no family, Peter. When I was seven, my parents were killed in a railway accident. I was sent away by an autocratic uncle I hardly knew and registered as a cadet at a demanding military school in East Prussia."

"How was it?"

"Brutal," Lang said, giving Peter a gallows laugh. "But we were taught strict discipline, and this has served me well."

"I know what it is like not to have parents around," Peter mused. "My father abandoned us when I was young. My mother worked and didn't have much time for my brother and me. We never see each other any more—too many shared bad memories I suppose. I haven't had much experience with family life, either."

There was a long silence between the two men before Lang spoke again, grimly, but without self-pity.

"Peter, I find that some memories are better pushed away and buried. The Tuareg are my family." Lang paused, then his face broke into a surreptitious smile and he asked, "Do you know Nietzsche?"

"No, who is that?"

"A German philosopher who stated there is a will to power by the strong over social impotence and decadence. It is the responsibility of the superior races to govern and teach those who would otherwise remain at the lower levels of society."

"This guy sounds like a crackpot." Peter replied ungraciously. "Conquer others and destroy their traditions. Is this how you feel about the Tuareg?"

"Ach, Peter," Lang cried, "you Americans are so naive! Nietzsche was a giant. I have great admiration for the Tuareg and wish to do all I can for them. As a German officer, it is my duty to help provide for the greater good of these people." Lang stood up and looked down at Peter. "Nietzsche would have approved of the Tuareg because they are strong-willed and do not believe that fate controls their destiny."

Peter nodded, forcing a tight smile, but not responding further. He decided that it would be best to drop the subject. He had learned that any criticism of Lang's firm beliefs created antagonism, causing the German to feel personally threatened and often leading to an explosive tirade. Peter considered how he had seen Lang conducting arithmetic lessons with the Tuareg children using a sandstone wall as a blackboard. If this was the influence of Nietzsche, so be it.

A few weeks later, Peter was invited to attend a tribal festival to be held under three large tents that had been joined together for the occasion. When Peter arrived, he was placed between

Zohar and Lang. On either side of them were the men of the tribe who were seated opposite the women. Some of these women were playing musical instruments. Occasionally, people got up and danced with rapid, undulating motions and then sat down to make room for others. Through the dim light, Peter looked at the expressive faces of the Tuaregs around him and felt a magnetic energy within their circle.

As Peter listened to the music, he noticed two of the women used hollowed-out gourds covered by goat hide as drums. Another also used a gourd positioned at her knees, but with horse-hair strings attached to the opening which she played as a fiddle. There were also women playing small metal cymbals, bamboo flutes and ringing bells of different tones. They all wore wrapper-skirts and bolero-style embroidered blouses.

Zohar leaned toward Peter. "Mr. Ordway, you should know all our tents are the property of the women and they are in charge of what goes on inside them; this music, the preparation of food, making clothing, and dispensing herbal medicines, since they are our doctors."

"They play all these instruments rather than the men?" Peter asked the chief.

"Yes, our women are the caretakers of the old faith, the myths, legends, and songs of the tribe."

"Ja, and they sing beautifully!" Lang broke in. "Except that I have been unable to teach them to sing 'Lili Marlene.'"

Zohar laughed politely, clearly aware that joking was Lang's way of relaxation. He was glad the German was enjoying himself and turned again to the American.

"Mr. Ordway, you may have guessed that tonight is a special occasion. There is a courting ceremony going on in front of you. Notice that my son is sitting directly behind Marsaya."

Peter had wondered why Tafik was seated behind one of the women who was playing a flute. Marsaya's curly, dark hair was uncovered, as was the custom for an unmarried woman. She was most attractive with her eyelids accented by powdered black stone. Marsaya seemed a little flustered in her playing, and once she glanced back to give Tafik a furtive smile.

"Why is Tafik sitting behind her?" Peter inquired.

"It is the custom of the Tuareg," Zohar replied. "A man will sit behind the woman he wants during a gathering such as this for an hour or so. If he receives no encouragement, he returns to where the men are seated."

"I do not believe Tafik will have to rejoin us this evening," Lang remarked blandly.

"It is the women who select their husbands," Zohar continued, "and we are a monogamous people."

During the course of the evening, Peter realized that one of the older women serving food was especially attentive to Lang. He had observed her devotion to the German's well-being before and learned that her name was Dassine. Later that night, Peter asked Lang for a chess game. He was restless. Watching Tafik and Marsaya had stirred up memories of Claire. He wanted to unwind, but he found it hard to concentrate on the game.

"Ernst," Peter ventured after a while, "it seems to me that Dassine has a fondness for you, or is this just my imagination?"

"Ach, Peter!" Lang said with obvious discomfort. "She is a widow who is simply being kind to me. I have known her for years

and helped her after her husband was killed by my side in battle at the Hoggar."

"Well, Ernst, would it be such as bad thing to encourage Dassine…to become your wife?"

"Peter, I do not like this conversation," the German snorted
dismissively. "I have no such romantic thoughts. I do not require
these emotional attachments. It is a responsibility I would not
accept. I have no affinity for women, never have. They are an
enigma to me. You go too far with your assumptions."

"I'm sorry, I didn't mean to intrude. I guess I'm preoccupied
tonight with a woman in Algiers that I miss a great deal."

"I cannot help you in this discussion, Peter. Let us finish our
game," Lang said with finality.

One day Peter found Lang hoisting himself on a rope pulley
out of a deep well in the canyon and shaking his head in disgust.

"What's the problem, Captain?"

"I cannot perform any further reconstruction on this well,
Peter. We are running out of water, but if we go further down
there will be a cave-in. Also, the lower caulk base is becoming
harder to dig through."

Peter peered into the hole, which he thought must be over
sixty feet deep.

"You have done a remarkable job, Ernst."

"Come over here and feel these walls, Peter," Lang said, dropping to his knees beside the well. "They are reinforced by hot clay,
a burned mixture of gypsum and sand combined with basaltic
rocks gathered from the upper canyon."

Peter stroked a hand over the cool wall of the well and again
complimented the German on his work.

"Ach, no easy task with primitive tools, believe me, my friend," Lang boasted. "However, our stay here is nearly over. We must find new sources of water elsewhere."

Peter perked up and spoke too quickly. "Does this mean the tribe will be moving on soon?"

Immediately, Lang grew suspicious. Cautiously choosing his words, he said. "Yes, but as nomads they welcome movement."

Peter responded with deliberate ambiguity.

"Oh, well, I suppose they know where they must go."

The German could not resist this opening.

"As a matter of fact," Lang volunteered, "I will be leaving with a scouting party tomorrow morning on an important reconnaissance mission."

Peter laughed to himself. To Lang, all departures from camp represented military reconnaissance patrols of one sort or another. Maybe this meant he would be given his freedom soon.

"You know, Captain, I like these people and they have been good to me, but I'll be glad to go. I'm going nuts from the monotony," Peter declared with bitter emphasis.

The German gave Peter a disapproving look as if this statement by the American was a personal affront.

"For a prisoner of war, you have been given exceptional latitude by us, Lieutenant," Lang declared reproachfully. "The Tuareg are tenacious fighters, but they have tolerance and compassion. A fine people, Ordway, straightforward and honorable. They never break their bonds of trust. Each day you become more acceptable to them. Once you earn their respect, you gain their confidence. Do not ruin this by becoming disgruntled and making trouble, or there will be changes in your situation."

Peter stared off into space, not responding. There was a long silence, broken only by the far off bleating of goats. The flyer then looked at the German, who was standing ramrod straight in front of him, as if at attention.

"Tell me, Captain," Peter inquired, "don't you ever miss Germany?"

Lang, relaxed a little and rubbed his chin. His countenance took on a glazed detachment and when he responded again his annoyance at Peter had dissipated.

"I miss books to read, my phonograph music of Wagner, drinking schnapps, having bockwurst to eat," Lang said, "but to be frank, I had no real feelings for the people of my country who were not soldiers."

"Well, I miss my friends," Peter said resentfully.

"Lieutenant, one loses a sense of time out here—you are learning this. It is hard at first not to count the days, yet after a while you will cease to do this because it is pointless. The days are suspended because desert time is slow time when there is no combat. However, this allows for long, uninterrupted periods of reflection and planning for the future. It is my patriotism for Germany which sustains me. I don't need to be in Germany, Peter. My lack of personal comforts mean nothing. The Afrika Korps teaches one self-sacrifice. This is the attitude you should have as a pilot officer in this theater of war."

The two men separated and Peter walked slowly up to the rim of the canyon where he could look out at the desert from above and be by himself. The day held a slight breeze that brought stinging sand. Yet, the abrasive hands of this wind also sculptured the Sahara in perfect symmetry. Peter looked at the ribbed spires of the dunes whose contours floated into one another, constantly changing shape, while retaining a permanent majesty. The dunes were limitless with a desolate splendor of order.

Peter's discussion with Lang about friends and home had again brought memories of Claire and the intimacy of her companionship. Since his arrival at Camp Calle, the pilot's mind was absorbed by the desire to regain all that he had lost, particularly Claire. He knew she had given him up for dead and probably moved on with her life. Peter realized he had taken her love too much for granted. Even if he eventually came out of the desert, would she still feel the same toward him, or had he lost her forever? The idea tormented him. Lang was right about having time to think. With so much solitude and isolation in this timeless place, Peter had come to know himself better than before the crash. His values had altered, and the thing he valued most was Claire. To cope with his feelings of depression, Peter had resolved to try and not brood too much on the past and to live for each day by doing what he could to help around the camp. Peter felt something higher than himself was testing him, and he wanted to pass the test by learning to appreciate being alive.

Lang was gone for over a month. All Peter knew was that his party headed east out of Camp Calle. This was the opposite direction from where Peter wanted to go. A few weeks after the German left, another small caravan departed to the south. What did this mean? Shortly thereafter, Zohar sent for Peter with an offer to dine with him in his tent.

During the meal Zohar talked about small matters connected with life in the camp. Peter refrained from asking Zohar about

his release because he knew his silence would be more respected by the chief. It was better to stay on other topics at this point.

"I am curious about the fact that members of your tribe do
not pray to Allah." Peter said as the meal ended.

"Are you a religious person, Mr. Ordway?" Zohar inquired.

"Not particularly, not really," Peter responded.

"Allow me to explain that we are not Muslims. Thousands of
years ago, our ancestors lived along the North African coast of the
Mediterranean. We were here before Carthage and Rome. We
believe we are the descendants of Phoenician traders. Since the
Arab invasions of North Africa in the seventh century, we have
traveled southward in a long series of migrations, where we have
fought with Arabs, Turks, and European invaders. Many Berbers
have converted to Islam. Our clan has not. We retain the old ways."

"Then what are your religious beliefs?" Peter asked.

"For us, both good and evil spirits exist everywhere and their
existence must be acknowledged. For instance, when enjoying a
good fire, we may conduct a series of incantations to allow the
flames to carry into paradise any lost souls of our brethren. We
have dances of exorcism to drive away evil spirits. We sing songs
to the date palms, pray to water, give homage to a fine camel—
these all have good spirits. Our gods are desert gods who may
choose to help or hinder us."

"I have heard your men wear veils to keep evil spirits out of
their mouths, but why not the women?" Peter asked.

"Because traditionally, they do not think it is necessary, although
there are other benefits such as keeping the sand out of your mouth
on caravans. Even so, the women are stronger and more resistant
to evil spirits, you see." Zohar smiled with amusement.

Neither man spoke for a moment, and Zohar felt the turmoil within Peter. The old chief was aware that this tall American was much leaner and more introspective than when he had been brought to him nearly three months earlier.

"Mr. Ordway, we believe that whatever we do must encompass all our heart. To understand the heart one must have a communion with the silence of the inner spirit. Do you not believe living in the desert has affected you in this way?"

"I think it has, Zohar, and part of this has been due to your generosity in allowing me to adjust here among you."

"It is good of you to say this to me. Mr. Ordway, I want to also say how especially pleased I am by your excellent progress with our Captain Lang."

"Thank you," Peter said, thinking to himself that he actually missed the crazy bastard.

"Now it is my turn to keep up my end of our bargain. Soon I hope to have good news for you. While our caravans are engaged in trading for the staples we need—such as rice, millet, sugar, and dried mutton—one of our caravans is also attempting to make arrangements to take you to an area which crosses a trade route of other caravans where you can be transferred. Once this has been accomplished, we will break from this camp, which can no longer sustain us. In the meantime, you will be traveling and nearing your own people."

Peter knew the wily old chief had delayed his release until the time when Camp Calle would be deserted. This provided insurance against the pilot finding the Tuareg in case any interested authority persuaded him to try and locate the oasis in the future. During his stay, Peter had only heard two planes far off in the distance, no doubt on their way to remote airstrips covered with sand, weeds, and mud huts. This was not a region of air traffic. Zohar need not have been concerned. Moreover, Peter would never have betrayed his benefactors.

Zohar unrolled a cowhide map and asked Peter to update the current pipeline locations, airfields, and expanding human settlements in the Algerian-Libyan border area. The American saw no harm in giving Zohar information which was common knowledge because he was convinced Zohar wanted to keep his distance from regions to the west. When Peter was finished, Zohar thanked him and stood up.

"Mr. Ordway, I have a suggestion. Why don't you assume the teaching of mathematics with Captain Lang's students until he returns. Kondi can serve as your translator."

"I'd be happy to do so. It would keep me busy," Peter said. "Do you mind if I try to teach them some English phrases as well?"

"Not at all," Zohar replied.

Knowing he had a good chance of finally getting out sustained Peter through the long days ahead. He developed a regimen of teaching in the morning and helping with camp work, since many of the men were gone. He tended the camels, cut up the small supplies of palm wood into pieces and hauled water. After light lunches of bread and cheese—there was rarely any meat and he was always hungry—Peter napped during the searing white heat of the afternoons. Late in the day he hiked around the rim of the canyon where the soil was hard packed. He enjoyed the serenity of the oasis then, watching the colors of the dunes around the camp change from a golden pink into deep purple with the angles of the setting sun. Once in a while he took short camel rides with Kondi. The boy was bright, and often in the evenings Peter taught Kondi

English while improving his own Arabic. Every night Peter would sit outside under the stars evaluating his life—and waiting.

At last the caravans returned, about a week apart, with Lang and Tafik coming first. Long conferences followed, and Peter wondered what was going on. The first evening, Lang entered Peter's tent bristling with excitement and anticipation.

"Peter, our new camp will be in a mountain stronghold with plenty of palm trees, game, and water, but what is more important is the likelihood of engagements with British troops from Egypt!"

"Oh, further to the east," Peter observed.

The German soldier froze, realizing that he had given too much away in his enthusiasm. This is what comes of being too friendly with the enemy, he thought. Lang's face twitched in frustration as he mulled over his commandant's reaction to revealing deployment intelligence to an Allied officer. Peter scrutinized the German, knowing all too well the implications of these emotional signs. They had to be diffused.

"Ernst, I will say nothing. I am glad you told me that the camp will be moved to a better place. We are running short of food and fuel here. It is causing hardship for the women and children."

Lang was somewhat mollified, but he chose to leave Peter, nonetheless. For some nights their chess games were not renewed. Peter overheard an older boy telling Kondi about their destination to the east. He caught the word Korizo, which was all he needed to know. The tribe was going through the Korizo Pass, probably into the extensive mountain canyons of the Tibesti in the border region of Libya and Chad. He had flown over this area once, and it truly was a vast warren of mountains over 150 miles across.

Zohar sent for Peter at last.

"Mr. Ordway, we are ready for you to be taken by a small party south to the Bilma caravan trail. Do you know of it?"

"Only that the trail crosses into Niger. God, that's a long way from the westerly direction I had hoped for."

"It is necessary for our security," Zohar said flatly. "Do not be concerned. This trail connects with the northwest trail to Gnat in Algeria. My men will see to it that you join a caravan proceeding to this town, where you will be safe. All this will take some weeks, however. I will send Kondi so you will have someone to talk to."

"Sir, I appreciate all your trouble," Peter said.

"Mr. Ordway, you can show that gratitude by granting me a personal favor. There are members of my council who did not want you to survive in order to protect our Captain. I judge you to be a man of trustworthiness. I want your word you will never tell the outside world of the whereabouts of Captain Lang."

"You have it, sir," Peter said sincerely. "I had already decided it would be best not to do so."

Zohar voiced his concerns to the American.

"Well-meaning officials from his country would mount a serious expedition to find the Captain for humanitarian reasons, not understanding that a return to Germany would destroy him. You see this?"

"Of course I do," Peter said reassuringly. "You have my solemn promise. He has become my friend. I owe him my life."

This last statement by Peter satisfied Zohar more than what had gone before between them. With great dignity the seasoned warrior shook Peter's hand.

"*Au revoir, effendi.* Peace be with you. Be ready to leave at dawn."

That evening Peter went around the camp saying his goodbyes and received hugs from some of the women and handshakes from the men. Palm wine was passed around while the men toasted this resilient American who had lived among them for a time. Lang participated in the proceedings with a strange detachment.

The next morning, Lang came to Peter wearing his ragged military tunic, so incongruent with a pair of goatskin boots. On his head was a frayed campaign hat, peaked in front, which held a set of pockmarked desert goggles. Months ago, Peter would have laughed. Not now. As for himself, Peter wore a burnoose, the hooded cloak draped as a toga over his own clothes. With this costume, Peter felt he must look like Lawrence of Arabia.

"I thought I should be properly dressed in honor of your departure, Lieutenant," Lang said, sadness in his voice. Then he smiled. "Also as a reminder for you to avoid being shot down again over my territory. I might not be around to rescue you."

Peter took the German's hand warmly, then stepping back, he saluted.

"Captain Lang, I would like to salute a man of chivalry—a fine soldier—a survivor of the 21st. Farewell. I will never forget you."

For the first time since he had known him, Peter saw tears in the old veteran's eyes. They waved to each other as Peter's camel ambled away from the camp with Kondi and three other Tuareg. The boy was chattering happily in his excitement with the assignment of being one of Peter's escorts. Peter's attention was elsewhere. He turned in his saddle for a last glance at his captor standing on top of a high dune, sunlight glinting off his military goggles. Captain Lang had already turned away from Peter's direction and was looking eastward, his mind on the next campaign.

Finite

ENTRY #1VOLUME #336 CATALOG #120069

Y NAME IS KOLAM, last historian of the human race. This final entry will summarize the chronicles of our accomplishments and is filed on top of other magnetically recorded testaments in this vault. We have placed a permanent laser beacon in a tower directly above ground as a marker on this planet of our origin. It is a meaningless formality. We wish to share our knowledge only with worthy successors, although we know that no other beings with the means of reaching this solar system can equal our intellectual and technical power.

Nine million, seven thousand years have passed since we emerged from the caves of this ancient world at the dawn of our civilization. We survived the forces of nature, overcame disease, pestilence, and the love of war between our kind to reach for the sky.

The way to the stars was paved with disillusionment, failures, and death, yet overcoming the hazards of space travel sustained our race in the same manner as when our exploration was limited to this planet we call Earth.

As interstellar travel began, we pushed outward to those stars nearest Sol, our sun. Traveling beyond, toward the core of our galaxy, faster spacecraft were developed capable of reaching the speed of light. When this proved to be too slow we condensed space and time by building ships equipped with hyperspace drives that facilitated rapid jumps between galaxies. Our exploration teams found that only one sun out of hundreds was composed of single star systems which could support planetary life. Among these, only one planet out of thousands was at all suitable for our species.

The quest for new habitable worlds was relentless. Planets were sought out, colonized and usually our race prospered anew under different sets of conditions. Challenges were met, conquered and our influence expanded further into the abyss of space. The journey was long and arduous. Out of almost ten million years of history, all but the first million years and the last three thousand were spent on other worlds.

Our race tracked across monstrous distances to build other galactic empires. We arrived in regions where alien life forms existed, some with subtleties of intelligence exceeding our own. Competition, when it came, was welcomed if non-combative. Anything we construed to be a menace to our society was suppressed because we are a proud race with the need to dominate. Most of the intelligent beings we found were either physically too frail to withstand the rigors of space travel or lacked the mental desire for exploration outside their own worlds. When we met powerful races with space travel proficiencies, we considered them to be a threat. They were either conquered into submission or destroyed. With other more peaceful empires, we established non-interference treaties for those areas we wished to populate.

Human beings alone were endowed with the insatiable curiosity, fierce determination and ingenuity necessary to populate all the cosmos. The dreams of humans could only be satisfied by continual movement and discovery of the unknown. Restlessness, and the hunger for environments which presented danger, was always part of human nature. The obsession for expansion proved to be our undoing.

The start of our decline can be traced to the day of The Discovery. The event which all our people thought would never happen, did happen. On the seventh day, forty-first year, sixteen-thousandth sequence of the ninth cycle, the exploration ship Prometheus IV, plying its way through the Monsar Cluster reported an unusual phenomenon. This particular section of Galaxy 878 M.C.H., which was supposed to be virgin territory, was already charted.

Reducing down to an operational speed of sub-space drive, the ship's captain double-checked his navigator's startling findings. There was no mistake. All the star systems in this sector had been recorded centuries before, duly registered on celestial charts and stored in the ship's memory banks.

Other, larger ships were called into the sector, probing, analyzing and coordinating their findings with the galactic center of this entire region. The results were indisputable. Within a decade the terrible truth was confirmed by reports from all our other fleets in the universe. Numerous cosmologists among us—like those early geographers who thought the sphere of Earth was flat—believed space to be flat as well. They were wrong. The universe was not infinite. We found it curved back on itself in a gigantic sphere. Our universe is inside the fabric of an expanding and contracting bubble that will not allow us to break through its walls. We had gone to the limits of our living space and did not have the ability to cross into other dimensions, if indeed they exist at all. The human race was now contained.

This basic, cruel truth was one which we should have realized was possible and been psychologically prepared to meet. However, the spirit of our adventuresome people was crushed by the knowledge that we had no more frontiers to conquer. Eventually, there was nothing left for our great technologies to bring under control. Humans were no more than a single protozoa swimming around the stagnant pond of our known universe. This ego-shattering principle brought a kind of madness and we changed, although not in the beginning.

The golden age of exploration lasted for another thousand years while we searched out every corner of space which had not been thoroughly examined. We even attempted to colonize worlds whose environments were so hostile it was impossible to sustain life. Failures mounted and out of sheer frustration the worst aspects of our nature were unleashed by renewed savagery among our own people.

We turned inward and in all our crowded citadels, spawned on thousands of worlds, people tore at each other over their confinement. The Discovery squeezed out the joy of life for teeming populations looking for exclusive places to exist. Our species was unable to find internal harmony. Worlds were demolished by endless wars and galaxies abandoned while we retreated back across the void of space toward the place of our origin. Finally, after we grew weary of fighting and the destruction was complete, our collective minds grew lethargic. Without challenges we became decadent. There was a lack of incentive, so vital to our race, and we lapsed into complete apathy.

While our space armadas fell into disuse, the vacated crystalline towers in millions of the mightiest cities crumbled into ruin. Human beings searching for that which was lost continued a slow withdrawal homeward. Eventually, the last remnants of countless generations of our race came back to the aged light of Sol and our cradle of Earth to die. At the beginning of colonization in this galaxy, Earth had become uninhabitable with total devastation of our oceans, land and atmosphere. We returned to a barren world and must end our days living underground breathing artificial air.

There are no more young people among us since the will to procreate is gone. The few of us who remain prefer a quick and painless death to a purposeless existence. We ponder one question among ourselves. If our species started over with the knowledge we have acquired about our universe, would the basic substance and final outcome of our existence have been different? Probably not. We were unable to eradicate our arrogance, intolerance and violence because we were not introspective as a race during our long expansion. We became the greatest civilization in the universe and yet we allowed ourselves to be ruled by the primitive nature of our biological bodies and did not change. We are what we were in the beginning.

Three stick-like biped creatures stepped back from the stack of magnetic plates piled high in the tomb. The leader emitted a short series of clicking noises inside his space helmet. He removed a heavy collection of journals and tucked them under his spindly appendage. The space travelers were in a hurry to leave this dying, inhospitable world revolving around a star located far out in a sparse, unimportant rim of this galaxy. They had to return to their mother ship soon in order not to be late in reaching the shifting vortex in this quadrant of space that would take them back to their own dimension. Time had been lost by the need for careful particle-stream blasting from a cannon mounted in their scout craft before the team could gain entrance to the sealed monument. The edifice had been almost impossibly fused by heat into the surrounding volcanic rock. Once inside, there was another obstacle. Their pathway to the vault was blocked by a panel of doors constructed of a material impervious to their equipment. To open them, it had been necessary to solve a series of complex mathematical symbols. They took what records they could from this strange race of people. Teams of linguists would work on the translations later. It was time to leave this place of the dead.

To order additional copies of this book,
please send full amount plus $5.00 for
postage and handling for the first book and
$1.00 for each additional book.
Minnesota residents add 7.125 percent sales tax

Send orders to:

Galde Press

PO Box 460
Lakeville, Minnesota 55044-0460

Credit card orders call 1–800–777–3454
Fax (952) 891–6091
Visit our website at www.galdepress.com
and download our free catalog,
or write for our catalog.